# Wishful Thinking

## by

# Evie Sparkes

Maddie could make things happen….and not just the little things.

# Acknowledgements

*I dedicate this book to my lovely Dad.*

*Special thanks to my editor Philippa Willitts and my illustrator Johanna Russell.*

Wishful Thinking - Evie Sparkes ©
Rachel Sheridan
The Glove Factory Studios, BA14
6RL
www.eviesparkes.co.uk

This is a work of fiction. Names,
characters, organisations, places,
events and incidents are either
products of the authors imagination or
are used fictitiously.

hello@eviesparkes.co.uk

Cover art by Johanna Russell

Edited by Philippa Willitts

*I can't remember when it was that I gave up believing in magic. It's funny how you can forget stuff. It's all here, in my own words and written in my scrawly, barely legible handwriting. It's not much better now. Thank God for computers. It isn't much of a diary, a bit of a half-arsed effort really. I'd forgotten all about it.*

*Technically it isn't a constellation, but it was to me. It was beautiful, the Big Dipper. The image looking back at me from my bedroom ceiling still fascinates me. I could waste an hour easily, just looking up at it and considering what else is up there or out there.*

*I often used to find myself wondering if I was actually the biggest geek at St. Stephen's. I was a contradiction because I wanted to be like everyone else, really. I fought with myself all the time. How would I ever get a boyfriend, or any more friends even, if I carried on being me?*

*Holding the little pink box again, I smile to myself. I'm not sure when I'd suddenly decided it was all nonsense. I remember feeling immense possibility back then, before I started to grow up and become all rational and... well, like everyone else, I suppose. I open it up to see a neat little pile of folded white paper. I smile to myself as I open up one from the top.*

*I remember how I felt, the day before everything changed. I am back there in my mind, that day that seemed so much like every other day. It's quite vivid as I lay looking up at my favourite star pattern again. I relax on my old bed, sinking my head into the feather pillows, letting the memory of teenage me gently wash over me.*

Chapter One

I kept getting this feeling in my stomach.
Well, it was sort of there but not. I say that
because, as soon as I tried to describe it to
myself, it disappeared, and I thought that
maybe I was imagining it. I couldn't explain
it, really. It had been niggling me for a few
days. It wasn't exactly bad or anything. Just
different. I supposed it was another of my
funnyisms, as Sophie called them.

I was disappointed when I pulled back the
curtains to see mostly cloudy skies and grey
clouds, too. Not even the fluffy white kind.

The weather forecast had showed the sun
symbol by itself the night before and they
usually showed a cloud, too, if they weren't
absolutely sure it was going to be really
sunny. I'd laid out my denim shorts and my
favourite oversized t-shirt at the end of my
bed and everything.

Now it looked like it might even rain.
There was a big, black cloud moving towards
us. Before I knew it, there it was, right over
our little white cottage. Gran was outside
resting her hands on her hips, the way she did
when she was thinking about doing

something. She'd just pegged the washing out and now she was thinking about taking it all back in again in case it got drenched in some random downpour that God had decided should replace the promised sun-soaked Tuesday.

It was the first proper day of the summer holidays. I had a whole day planned and those plans did not work in the rain.

Sophie didn't do rain. She wouldn't come out if there was the slightest chance of it because her hair was almost afro when it got wet. Her Dad was from Jamaica, but she'd never met him because he was already married to someone else when he got her Mum pregnant. Sophie said she was going to go and find him when she was eighteen, but Mrs. Guthrie said he might be dead by then because he took drugs and drank too much vodka.

Sophie was the prettiest girl in year nine. She had soft, tanned skin and her eyes were an unusual pale blue, even for a completely white person, let alone someone of mixed race. She had long, slim legs and she'd just started wearing a bra. I pretended I didn't care but, really, I was longing to buy one because it was embarrassing to not need one at my age.

Sophie said I should just get one anyway and stuff some socks down it, but I didn't want to just pretend to be entering into puberty. Gran said she was almost sixteen before she got her first bra. She was trying to make me feel better because I was the last girl in my class to get my period. We had a talk about teenage pregnancy at school a few weeks before and when the lady asked if everyone had their period now, I nodded along with everyone else. Secretly, I was worrying it might never come and I might never be able to have children. I don't know why I was worrying though, because I didn't even think I wanted any really.

I'd never even met my Mum and, as far as I was aware, I didn't have a Dad. I did, of course, because everyone does, but I didn't wonder about who he was or anything. He just didn't seem important. I was just ten weeks old when Mum died. Gran brought me up on her own. I had one picture. The house where she lived with Grandad had an electrical fault and there was a fire. Everything was burnt to ash. The picture I had was one that she gave me that Grandad used to keep in his wallet. I wasn't in it, though. It was of Mum sat on a wall somewhere I didn't recognise. It was the year before I was born, Gran said.

I kept it in my underwear drawer, but I didn't look at it often now. I used to stare at it and try and imagine what she was like and how she must have loved me, but I couldn't. I didn't feel anything. She was a stranger to me and Gran never talked about her really, and I didn't want to upset her, so I rarely asked anything.

The big black cloud had gone. Just like that, it disappeared to be replaced with bright blue skies just like the weather man had said. There were a few white clouds scattered about but nothing like the grey ones a few minutes before. It was almost as if they had disappeared just like that, or they had never really been there in the first place and I only dreamt them. I contemplated magic as I always did when things like that happened and I looked over at the little pink box that used to be Mum's. It had 'My wishes' written on it in gold swirly print. I'd never put anything inside of it, because, well, it seemed childish to do so. Gran gave it to me on my tenth birthday. She said she never knew where it came from, but that Mum had always kept it on her dressing table. She had kept her earrings in it Gran said. I'd always imagined it to be more than just a jewellery box. Stupid, really.

Every time I thought about magic, something crap followed my musings and I was nudged back into reality. About half an hour before I opened the curtains, I got filled with fear that it wouldn't be a nice day like they forecast after all and Sophie would refuse to come out of the house and into town with me. I had that feeling again. So, I was almost expecting it to be rubbish when I opened the curtains. After a few minutes of being crazy mad at the stupid weather man for being so adamant it would be wall-to-wall sun when he clearly had no right to make such a promise, I thought there's nothing I can do about the weather and resigned myself to the fact that it might rain, and I'd have to re-schedule the shopping trip. That's when the skies cleared.

It wasn't as if I had anyone else. Sophie didn't care that I was weird. She said she liked it that I wasn't like everyone else. She said I was fascinating, which made me blush bright red. She said it was a compliment and I suppose it was, but I didn't want to be different. It was just that I didn't know how not to be. I felt like I was hiding in the body of someone I didn't recognise. Like really, I was someone completely different and not Maddie Beaven at all.

When I thought about it, I was lucky to have Sophie because if I didn't, then what would I do with myself? I didn't have SnapChat or any of those other things because I didn't want people to make fun of me or, worse still, to see that I didn't have a fun-packed life.

I couldn't very well pretend because it's not as if people didn't know me. They'd have known I was lying and they'd probably have just laughed at me and called me sad.

No, it was better all-round if I stayed away from social media. I really didn't like it but part of me wanted to be like everyone else and have it just to fit in a bit more. Sophie kept going on at me and said so what if I didn't post stuff, at least I could see what everyone else was doing.

A new girl had started in our class a few weeks before the end of term. I thought maybe she might sit next to me because there was a spare seat. Danny Miles used to sit next to me, but he'd moved to Bristol. Sophie wasn't in my tutor group. She was in Mr. Hammond's class. He was young and fashionable and most of the girls in my class fancied him. I didn't think he was anything special. He tried too hard to be everyone's friend instead of being teacherish like he should have been.

Anyway, Miss Peterson sat the new girl next to Trudy Price instead. I couldn't help feeling disappointed because she'd smiled right at me when she was introduced to us. Her name was Penny Goodwood. She had one of those smiley faces and when she grinned, her whole face seemed to light up. Miss Peterson told us that she'd just moved from France where her Dad was working as a lecturer at a university or something. Anyway, that chance had gone. She'd got all friendly with Trudy and she was way popular. I didn't stand a chance.

'But it's my birthday on Saturday. Gran gave me twenty-five pounds. I wanted to spend it in TopShop!'

'Sorry Mads. It's just that Mum is making me take Tiegen to a party. She's got an early shift and, well, you know what she's like about stuff like that. We can do it another day. Not tomorrow though because I have to go to the dentist in the morning and then I have to meet Mum for lunch.'

So, that was that. I'd been ditched in favour of a five- year old's party. I knew I shouldn't have thought it, but I couldn't help thinking she was lying. I felt bad though, because Sophie wasn't like that.

I didn't know what to do. Gran had offered to take me into town instead but how would that have looked? *I'll probably see girls from school and they'll know for sure that I am a sad loser with no-one apart from Gran to go into town with.* I thought.

I didn't know what it was about me. I mean, I looked pretty normal on the outside. Actually, I thought I was sort of pretty. Sophie said I was and she didn't lie about stuff like that. I always made an effort to do something interesting with my hair, even for school. I didn't wear makeup, though, because it brought me out in spots. Although Gran did buy me one of those Nivea sticks for chapped lips that had a pink tint to it. I thought it made me look older, fifteen maybe.

It was just on the inside I was different. It was like there was something I was supposed to be doing that I had forgotten, or I was missing some part of me. Like there should have been something else and it just wasn't there. Oh, I don't know. It's hard to explain. Actually, it's impossible to explain because it was nonsense obviously. I was defective. Something about me wasn't right and I didn't know how to make it right.

We'd just finished tea. Gran had made cottage pie, which I didn't really care for all that much, but I'd never said, so she made it every Tuesday. We had apple crumble for pudding and then I had a hot chocolate. We watched The One Show and then Gran fell asleep. *What an absolutely crap start to the summer*, I thought, as I threw the last gloopy bit of chocolate down my throat. *I don't suppose tomorrow will be any better either*, I sighed to myself at the injustice of it all.

Reality was rubbish. I didn't like mine one bit at the moment. I wanted something to happen, something exciting that was all about me, only I had no idea what that might be.

Nothing exciting had ever happened to me, not ever. I was the invisible girl. People walked past me at school and I was sure they couldn't even see me. If I put my hand up in class, I was passed over for someone else, even though they weren't even offering an answer. I banged my feet hard on the floor until they hurt sometimes just to make sure I was actually there. I'd once thought about making something up, telling everyone at school that my parents couldn't take care of me because they worked for MI5 and they didn't want to risk my safety by having me live with them. I didn't, because when you start a lie, you have to keep it up or you'll end up worse off because you'll be found out and then you'll have no friends and have to move schools. *Perhaps Mum or my Dad were like this and it's in my DNA or something*, I thought. I can't help being weird. It's not my fault, it's one of them that's done this to me.

I felt like something was waiting to happen, though. It was like there was something I needed to do and then everything would change for me, only I didn't know what it was, so I was destined to feel unfinished forever.

That was the best description I could find. I didn't know why I hadn't thought of it before. I was unfinished. Like a jigsaw puzzle with a bit missing. You can look and look and look and you know it's supposed to be there because it was new in the box, but it isn't, so the picture will remain faulty, incomplete. *Why can't I just be like everyone else?* I thought. *I just want to be noticed.*

## Chapter Two

I woke up at 2am with the strangest feeling in my stomach. I sat up and pushed both my pillows behind my head because the world had started to spin when I was lying flat. After a few minutes, I felt different. It was like I could feel every organ in my body vibrating, only it didn't feel wrong or scary or anything like that. I kept on breathing in and out and I was pretty sure I hadn't died. Actually, I felt more alive than ever. An excitement came over me. I felt I could do just about anything in that moment. Then, I started to feel desperate to keep the feeling because I didn't want to feel crap again. I liked the way I felt in that moment. After a few seconds of panic, I was okay. The calm was back, and I felt like maybe it was the missing bit of me. It had come to me in the early hours of Wednesday morning. My jigsaw was complete, I was right at last. At least that's how I felt in that moment.

Of course, all of that seemed ridiculous in the cold light of day. Or should I say the warm light of day. There wasn't one cloud in the sky that morning, not one. Even the sun looked bigger. Come to think of it, the grass looked greener, too, like that pretend stuff

Mr. and Mrs. Matthews had that Gran said cost them four thousand pounds, which seemed mental to me. Why would you pay all that money for grass when it grows for free?

'Let's go into town today, shall we?' Sophie called at nine. Her dentist had cancelled on her because everyone was off sick or something and her Mum was in bed with a migraine, so they weren't going for lunch. 'I'll buy you an early birthday lunch', she said.

She arrived at five to ten, that's a whole five minutes early, which in itself was a little miracle because she was always but always late. She didn't know how to be early. It was like she thought it wasn't important. I suppose it's not, really. I just hated waiting for things. Anything actually. Buses, waiting in queues, at the dentist, for Sophie... I wanted everything to happen now, right this minute.

Today, I felt happy. For the first time in as long as I could remember, I was properly happy. Gran called it contentment. I used to think How can anyone ever just be happy as they are? because there were too many things I wanted and now I didn't care about them. It wasn't as if I didn't want them or anything, more like it just wasn't important that I had them right then. I felt like I was surrounded by an invisible bubble of possibility. I felt invincible, like nothing could hurt me anymore. What on earth was happening to me?

Gran made us toast with butter and marmite and a cup of tea. She liked to feed Sophie because she said she was too skinny. She was slim, but she couldn't help it. She ate way more than me, but she never put weight on.

'What are you going to buy?', Sophie asked as I scoffed the last little bit of crust. 'Maybe we should go to Primark. You'll get more there.'

'Yeah, okay maybe.' I didn't care where we went. I was just pleased we were going. 'Have you got any money?'

'Nah.' She never had any money. Mrs. Guthrie didn't believe in giving her any so she had to do a paper round and then she had to pay for cat food and her bus fare out of her wages because Mrs. Guthrie said it was Sophie that wanted Pickles and she could just as easily walk to school as get the bus so why should she fork out for it just because she was lazy.

Town was unusually quiet. I always felt a bit uneasy when it was too busy. I got nervous a pigeon would fly at me and I wouldn't be able to avoid it because there would be too many Chinese tourists in my way or I'd get nudged off the curb and twist my ankle. It was really quite nice out. There were people around, but none of them seemed to be getting in my way and I hadn't seen a single pigeon so far. Sophie had linked my arm, which I liked but she hardly ever did it because she said I walked too slowly. Today, she seemed happy to do exactly what I wanted to do. She didn't even complain when I needed the toilet and we had to take the stairs to the top floor in Marks and Spencer because the lift was broken.

Usually, when things went right for me, I kept expecting them to go wrong until they eventually did. But, today, I didn't have that worry. It was a new experience for me. I wasn't quite sure what had happened to me and I was more than sure it wouldn't last but, until it wore off, I intended to enjoy every moment of this new Maddie. She was the one I always wanted to be. God, I hoped she wasn't a dream and I'd wake up any minute as the old me, in my bed only to hear the rain and wind battering the double glazing with zero hope of a day in town because Sophie would be going to the dentist after all and Mrs. Guthrie would be all chirpy and well.

I didn't let the fear take hold of me. There was no way I was going to ruin this perfect morning, not for anything.

'Maddie!' I heard a shriek come from the direction of McDonalds. I turned around sharply and there she was. Penny Goodwood, the new girl was calling out my name and I didn't even think she knew it. She was excitedly waving at me and beckoning us over.

'Hi!', I said, as we headed in her direction. 'Are you here with someone?' I didn't know what else to say.

'Yeah… well no actually. I was but not now.' She went a bit red. I think she'd been with Michael Mathers from year ten because I'd seen her with him. 'What are you guys doing?' She asked.

'Just hanging out', I replied, all casual. 'Want to join us?' I wasn't quite sure where that came from. Of course she didn't want to join us, 'I suppose you're busy though…'.

'Great, I'd love to, if that's okay?' She looked at Sophie, who looked at me like I'd just said the absolute worst thing ever in the history of worst things to say to someone who wasn't her.

'Yeah, no problem. If you want to', Sophie said. She didn't mean it, I could tell.

She was cross with me for asking another girl to share our day. I should have felt bad, but I didn't. It was alright for her, she didn't struggle to make friends like me. I had to take them where I found them. Anyway, Penny was nice, they'd get along fine.

It was turning out to be the best day ever. I popped into TopShop on the off chance there would be something I could afford with my twenty-five pounds that wasn't on the sale rack from last season and, to my complete surprise, there was the skirt I'd desperately been wanting since I saw it on Perrie from Little Mix. It was almost sixty pounds reduced to twenty- five! There was just one size eight and a size fourteen left. I grasped at it triumphantly as Sophie and Penny gasped. 'I absolutely love that', Penny said grabbing at my little black and gold treasure. 'Can't believe it's so cheap. Do you think it's a mistake?'

'It's my lucky day!', I shrieked like a ten-year old. I couldn't help it. It was like a domino effect of good things was happening. I was on a roll and nothing could stop me from getting everything I wanted.

'Don't you want to go to Primark?' Sophie asked. 'You'll get lots more if you do.'

'No way. This was meant for me. It's worth all my birthday money and then some.'

Why wasn't she excited for me, too? Penny was beside herself and she wasn't even my best friend.

'But where will you wear it? It's for parties isn't it? You don't go to parties. You don't like loud music.'

'When did I say that?'

'You always say it', she said, looking cross with me. 'That's why I have to turn it down when you come over. You have sensitive ears, you said.'

'Well, anyway, I'm more mature now aren't I? I'll be fourteen on Saturday.' I felt different. Maybe I was growing up. Maybe life was going to be like this from now on. I just had to keep this feeling inside of me all the time and everything would be good.

# Chapter Three

I woke up feeling the same as yesterday. I breathed a sigh of relief that I hadn't slipped back to the other, old version of Maddie.

The feeling inside of me was like nothing I can ever explain in words, not without sounding crazy. *I can be crazy though, that's okay, just not in public*, I thought. I wanted to shout it from the rooftops: 'MAGIC DOES EXIST!'. Everyone was missing out, believing it didn't and that it was only for the likes of Harry Potter movies. But, of course, I couldn't because I'd have ended up with no friends, Penny would have disappeared in a flash and even Sophie might have disowned me out of embarrassment. All of this would disappear. I can't feel bad, not ever again, I told myself. If I lose this feeling, then it will all go back to how it was.

'You're chipper this morning, love', Gran said as she poured half a cup of milk into my tea.

'Actually, Gran, I'd rather not have so much milk in my tea', I said. Usually I accepted everything the way it came and just moaned inwardly. 'If that's okay?'

'Of course, love.' She tipped it down the sink and made me another just the way I liked it. 'There you go.'

'Thanks, Gran.'

I could have said that before, I know that, but I just wouldn't have. I can't explain why, I told you I was weird, didn't I? Now things just came out. I knew that I could say them, and it wouldn't be the end of life as I knew it. I couldn't upset someone by asking them for less milk. How stupid that I ever thought I could.

I had discovered that, as long as I could feel good and not feel crap, then I could do and have anything. I did wonder when the genie that had bestowed this gift on me might appear and tell me what I had to give it in return for all these good things, but I didn't let it invade my head or anything and, actually, I might have given just about anything to keep it. I pulled out a note pad from my desk drawer and started writing.

*My Magic Wishes*

*To be really good friends with Penny*
*To be popular with all the girls in my class…*
*no, with everyone*

*To get a Saturday job*
*To be able to wear makeup and not get spots*
*For people other than Sophie to call me*
*pretty*
*To know more about Mum*
*To have a boyfriend by September*

There, that would do for now. *That last one might be a bit of a push*, I thought, but what the hell. I was sure there were loads of other things I might want, but they'd come to me later. I'd get these things first.

I didn't even worry that I wouldn't get them or that they wouldn't happen in good time, because I just somehow knew that they would. I wasn't even telling myself to stop being weird or anything. Weird had got me this far, so weird was not bad anymore.

I wondered if maybe Mum was a witch. It was possible that I had the witch gene. I'd made up my mind. I was going to ask Gran about her. I should have done it before. I think I just didn't want to upset her by talking about her dead daughter or making her feel like she wasn't enough for me.

I'd spent too much time worrying about upsetting people and not enough time caring about how I feel about things. Now, I could see that I was important too. I did matter, and I was going to stop putting myself last.

I picked up the pink box of Mum's. I dropped all of my wishes into it and stuffed it into the bottom of my wardrobe. I didn't want Gran to find it and look inside. That might break the spell and, anyway, it would be embarrassing.

I had no doubt at all that all of these things would happen. I had a rush of something inside of me. I couldn't explain it. It wasn't exactly excitement, but I didn't know how to describe it. I put all of my sort of, almost right words into Google and came up with 'momentum'. The perfect word. Momentum was whirling around inside of me. Where had it come from? Why had it picked me? I had no idea why this was happening to me and, on another day, I would have probably worried myself out of this amazing state. Somehow, I wasn't concerned that it wouldn't last or that I was dreaming, or that I'd slipped into a parallel universe. I didn't have the niggling doubt that had plagued me over just about everything in my entire existence until now. Perhaps the pink box was magic after all. Maybe it just had to be activated or something. Perhaps, when I was studying it the other day, I accidently touched the 'On' button.

I did consider telling someone. Well, Sophie, no-one else would even consider staying to listen after I mentioned the word 'magic'. But I decided perhaps telling someone might break the entire spell and that would be the end of all this.

Anyway, it was no-one else's business. Maybe I was supposed to keep it a secret. Maybe it was like some sort of test and I'd stuff it all up by telling someone. I looked up at the ceiling as if maybe God was looking down on me, wondering whether or not he'd given all of this power to the wrong person after all, like maybe it was meant for someone else and I got it by mistake or something.

Even if it only lasted a little while, it would still be better than never having had it at all, wouldn't it? If I at least got one of my wishes, then things would be better than before. I had no idea who I was writing my little wish notes to, or even if there was anybody answering me. Maybe it was really me. I was magic all by myself. It was in me all along and I just didn't know it. Maybe the missing piece really was this. It was lying dormant all of these years to be woken up by… what? God knows. Nothing special had happened the day before. Only the funny feeling in the early hours. That weird feeling that grew and grew and ended up as this, in me, now. Perhaps I'd been taken over by something alien, maybe it was growing inside of me and eventually it would take over entirely. Even that didn't scare me. So what? It wasn't as if I had anything I wanted to hang on to.

I fished out Mum's photo from underneath my rubbish knicker drawer. I'd never worried about such things as nice underwear before. I was only concerned with the parts people could see. Looking at the off-white pack of five short style briefs Gran always bought me, I made a decision to have more nice pairs. I decided I would have a bra by the end of the month and not just because I wanted one, but because I needed one. My breasts would grow in the next three weeks. I wrote it down and popped it into by wish box.

*I would like to have an A cup (or bigger) at the end of this month or maybe next month at least, and some nice knickers, like from Beau Avenue or somewhere similar.*

I had no money and, with the lack of a Saturday job (which I'd been desperately wanting for the last five months), I had no idea how this might happen. Then again, I didn't think I needed to know. It seemed that things seamlessly happened without much input from me.

When you're not even fourteen yet, it's hard to get anyone to take you on and you can only work a few hours even if they do. I tried the bakery on the High Street and some shops in town but they all said I was too young and they didn't take anyone under sixteen. I did not want a paper round. Not under any circumstances did I want to get up at ridiculous o'clock and suffer downpour upon downpour in a quest to give people something to read with their breakfast. Anyway, Sophie said the money's crap.

Mum doesn't look like me, I thought, as I studied my face in the mirror hoping to notice some similarities between us. But there was nothing. Gran said she used to draw stuff. I don't know if she was an artist or anything though. I think she was just good at arty things. Bloody hell, I can't believe I don't know more about her, I don't even know how old she was when she died.

All I knew was that she died in a car crash. Gran had never elaborated and, to be honest, I'd never really wanted to know how it happened. I'd never wanted to have an image of her bleeding and slowly dying while she waited for help to come that didn't arrive on time. Gran only had one child and Grandad died before I was born. She only had me now. I wished she'd get some friends so that I didn't have to feel so concerned about her all the time. It was stupid, really, because she didn't do anything to make me worry about her. She said she didn't need friends and didn't care to have any.

*I wish Gran would get a friend*

My little box was filling up. I hoped I wasn't being greedy. I didn't want to have my magic snatched away because I wanted too much. I tapped the lid. Right that's definitely it for now.

Gran brought me a cup of tea and a piece of cheese on toast for supper as I started writing. I wanted to document this, in case it all went away and my memory was scrubbed or something because it was just one big experiment by the government.

*Dear Diary, I don't understand what is happening to me and why. I get a little glimpse of the old me sometimes and I feel like maybe she's coming back. Maybe it's a warning that I don't have long left like this. I've stopped worrying about most things. I don't know how I've managed to do this, but I have. Why have I been chosen? I'm not anything special as far as I know. Was Mum like this?*

## Chapter Four

I woke up at eight precisely. Not half past, not quarter past, not even five-past. Eight, exactly as I had planned. It wasn't difficult to drag myself up like it usually was. Gran hadn't even got around to bringing me my toast and tea. When I said I was getting up at eight, she knew it wasn't humanly possible for me to actually get up at eight. She said there was something in my genes that meant I couldn't do things the easy or the proper way, I had to do things ass backwards, she said. I thought it was a stupid saying anyway. How could you do something ass backwards, because it was already backwards, you couldn't backwards an ass.

I wondered how long it would be before something cool happened. My momentum was still swishing around inside of me. It was filling every part of me today, not just my tummy like it had been the previous day. The part of me that would usually say, *right that's it, it must burn itself out at some point and maybe everything will end up being twice as bad when it eventually does…* well, that part of me was not there. Not much, anyway. She might have been peeking over the edge slightly, but she was not trying to pull herself up to be seen.

I slept with the photo of Mum that night. The more I looked at her, the more blurred her face became until I could barely make it out. How weird is that? It's like I couldn't focus on her. I think I kept looking at her because I hoped I might suddenly feel a bolt of something, like lightning inside of me that made me know that she loved me and I'd suddenly realise that I DO have her nose after all.

'Morning, love!'

Gran came in with a plate of toast and my tea. 'Blimey, you're already up. You off out somewhere, then? she asked, plonking it down on top of my diary. It felt sacred. I didn't want tea stains on it. I whipped it from under them and tucked it under my pillow.

'What's that then, a diary? Got your boyfriends in there have you?', she laughed.

'No', I snapped.

'Oh well love, there's plenty of time for all that. No need to rush.'

'Not interested anyway', I lied and took a bite of underdone toast dripping in salted butter. Perfect.

I liked Josh Howells from my maths class. We were only in that one class together and I didn't think he'd ever even looked in my general direction, let alone noticed me. He was too good looking for the likes of me anyway. He went out with Jessica Stephens in Sophie's class. She was probably the most popular girl in the whole of year nine and she was the eldest. She only just missed being a year ten. I only just missed being a year eight. I hated it that everyone else was fourteen already. Well, apart from Penny. It felt like we were meant to be friends. There was something about her I really liked. Probably the fact that she liked me I expect.

Penny was pretty, not Sophie pretty, but there was something about her. She had really blonde hair, that was cut into a sharp bob, and she had one of those long side fringes. The ones they show you how to cut on Youtube.

I thought she would be nice, because she always smiled at me when we passed each other in the corridor. Popular girls usually acted like I didn't exist, or maybe they didn't see me. It was like I blended into the paintwork or something. Penny was different. At first I thought that maybe she felt sorry for me, and that was why she used to smile. I don't think that's the reason now though.

I pulled on my jeans and the red halter neck top I'd found in the charity shop the day before for three pounds that was from River Island and still had the twenty pounds price tag attached and I surveyed myself in the full-length mirror. I was going to try and wear some makeup today. Just a bit to test my makeup-without-spots wish.

*Hi Maddie, I'm going to the cinema for my birthday next Friday. I'd really like it if you came along. :) xx*

I hadn't given Penny my number, well not that I could remember anyway. Would I come? Of course I bloody would!

*Hi Penny, thanks I'd love to come. ;) xxx*

Was that too much? That was one kiss more than she gave me and why did I do the winking emoji? Oh god, now she was going to regret asking me. I stared at my phone, willing her to reply and put me out of my misery. Nothing. Five minutes, ten minutes, fifteen. Shit, I'd messed up. So near and yet so far.

Throwing my phone onto the bed, I decided that was that.

*Oh well never mind*, I thought to myself. I might be able to pull it back some other time. I wasn't beside myself at ruining my one chance at another friendship like I would have been before. After the initial disappointment started to wear off, I made myself a hot chocolate and one for Gran before running back up the stairs ready to make another diary entry.

There it was: *Great, meet us outside of the cinema at 3 then. :)xxx*

Oh my God! She'd even matched my three kisses. I was beyond excited. I had another friend and not one that had been pressured into inviting me to her party by Sophie. I hoped she didn't think I hadn't invited her to mine. I was only going for dinner with Gran because I felt bad not being with her on my birthday. It didn't seem right somehow. We always spent the day together and then went for dinner. For as many years as I could remember. I think it was important to her. As much as I wanted to wish for a day with my two friends, I just couldn't bring myself to add that wish to the box.

*Dear Diary, Penny asked me to the cinema next week for her birthday! I'm a little bit nervous because I know other girls will be there, but not nervous enough not to go. So, I can tick one wish off the list. I have more than one friend Woohoo!!! So what if I don't understand what is happening to me? Does it matter? Can this really go on? I'm scared that if I think too much about how this is happening, it will be like I'm questioning this amazing thing and not trusting and so I'll get it snatched away.*

*Why do we have to have all of the answers anyway? I like the fact that I don't know what is happening or how, in a funny sort of way. When life was like it was before, it wasn't exciting. It was all about coincidence or fate and now it's about possibilities and the chance to be more and have more. I am so happy right now I could burst.*

I supposed this was happiness. I didn't have anything to compare it to I could only assume that's what I was feeling. It wasn't the momentum feeling, although that was there still. It was a sense of calm inside of me and a feeling that all was good with the world and, even if it wasn't, then it couldn't hurt me. When I actually thought those words, I felt a bit strange, like it was selfish of me not to care if things weren't well everywhere else. I mean, it wasn't like I didn't care for starving people in Africa or poor people, or worn-out donkeys and stuff. I just didn't feel like crying or rummaging through my piggy bank to find some spare change to put in the bucket at Morrisons.

'Shall we sit in the garden? I've made some lemonade and shortbread biscuits, the ones you like with the lemon', Gran said.

'Yeah, okay cool.' It was extremely hot and the thought of sharp fizzy bubbles on the back of my throat was totally appealing. 'I thought I might cook for you tonight, Gran', I said. I'd never done that before and I had an overwhelming urge to do something nice for her.

'Oh well usually that would be lovely but well… I'm going out', she replied, blushing the colour of her home-grown tomatoes.

'Are you?', I said. I could feel a rush of excitement. Wow, I just knew she was going to have made a friend. Oh my bloody god, two wishes in one day! 'Who are you going out with?'

'well… and there's nothing in this, not at all. I know you'll think otherwise but he's just a friend and well, I don't have any of those do I?'

She trailed off and looked at me. She had made a man friend? That's not what I had wished for. I didn't know how I felt about that. The thought that she might have a boyfriend had never entered my head. I didn't want some man here, taking over and telling me what to do. He'd probably say she fusses me too much and tell me off for being lazy.

'That's okay isn't it love? He's just a friend. He knew your Grandad years ago. You know, Grandad's best friend I was telling you about?'

'The one with the sweary wife?', I asked. 'Doesn't she mind?'

'Oh, she died, a couple of years ago now. He's lonely, I think', she said as she continued to look at me like the cat from Puss In Boots. How could I get all pissy with her? You could have man friends just like you could have women friends. Of course it was okay. *It'll be fine Maddie, everything will be fine*, I told myself forcefully. I couldn't very well wish a friend for her and then selfishly wish them away again just because they weren't what I was expecting, could I?

It had been a good day, yes, a really good day. It didn't matter that Gran had a potential boyfriend hanging about. When I came to think about it, she wouldn't want a man about the house anyway. She was always saying how she liked things done her way and she couldn't imagine having to compromise at her age. She'd got used to not having Grandad around now, she said. No, I didn't think I really had anything to worry about with Arthur. Like she said, he was probably just lonely, and his wife had only been dead a couple of years. *You should at least wait five years before marrying again or even getting a girlfriend,* I thought.

So yes, two wishes it was. In one day, too. At this rate, I could easily add some more to my wish box. I bet I could think of loads of things if I put my mind to it. It would be like doing a shopping dash in TopShop with an unlimited amount of time. You still want to dash around like a mental person because it adds to the excitement, even though you don't really have to.

## Chapter Five


*Oh my absolute word,* I said out loud. I had borrowed some of Gran's Body Shop foundation and it was my perfect colour. I had tried it the night before and I didn't wake up with one spot. I added a touch of mascara and some of my chapstick lipstick thingy. I pulled my hair up into a high pony tail and curled the length of it with my straighteners like I'd watched some girls do on Youtube. *No decent-sized breasts yet,* I thought as I cupped my pathetic offerings, but I couldn't expect everything at once. I looked pretty damn good, even if I did say so myself. It was almost wasted on Gran, though. She was taking me to lunch at Pizza Express and then dinner at Cafe Rouge. She let me choose. I first thought about the most out-of-town places I could, in case I saw someone I knew but then I thought: *Stuff it, I am invincible. No-one is going to take the piss out of me and if they do then I'll just stick my middle finger at them.*

Studying my face closely in the mirror, I decided I looked at least fifteen and maybe even sixteen. It was just the lack of anything under my top that gave the game away. Still,

I wasn't going to think about the things that weren't right, I was only going to concentrate on the good stuff. I thought the more I did that the more good things would happen. I couldn't believe I'd spent so much time worrying and thinking the worst, now. It seemed so stupid. What a waste of time and where had it got me? More of the same. *If you think negative, you get negative.* Bloody hell, was it really as simple as that? Was this absolute magic down to something as easy to explain? It surely couldn't be but, at the same time, I kind of had this feeling that it was. I've always had this fascination with science and I thought that contradicted my belief in magic, so I pushed the magic away because science is so much more grown up.

*Happy Birthday Maddie xxx*

A text from Penny! I had actually managed to wish myself a new friend. I was so happy at the moment that I could have burst. Was I becoming popular? What was Penny seeing in me that she hadn't seen before?

*Thanks :) x*

I decided to pull back a bit. I didn't want to seem too keen. There was always a chance that she might turn on her heels and run if she thought I was getting all clingy. That's not how it was, not at all, but I hadn't had any experience of friends, apart from Sophie. We'd been mates since primary school. She had found me crying in the toilets because I had been picked last for netball again. I was always picked last. Probably because I was rubbish at netball. That day, I just crumbled. I had no real friends by the time I was eight. All the friends I'd had in the infants had branched off and made best friends and found their little cliques, but I had somehow been left by myself. I wasn't even sure how it had happened. It was just like I'd been forgotten or something. Sophie had rescued me from years of the same. When I came to think about it, I had screamed to myself *I want a friend!*. I'd forgotten about that. Now that memory is so vivid.

### *Morning Maddie, have a lovely day. Hope you like your pressie! xxxxxxx*

I'd forgotten for a moment. It was my birthday. I was fourteen, almost an adult. I was growing into myself. That's what Gran used to say when I complained that everyone thought I was weird. You'll grow into yourself one day love, she'd say and I'd think, *what a stupid thing to say.* But it wasn't stupid because here I am... growing into myself.

I grabbed the little square package from my bedside table. Sophie always made things look pretty. She could sit and fold things neatly, add bows and write beautifully in italic. I bet it had taken her at least half an hour to make it look like that. It was wasted on me, of course. I tore it open and threw the pink happy birthday paper onto my bed. The little black velvet box excited me. I popped the hinged top open to reveal the most beautiful silver necklace. I opened the little heart. A photo of us both on each side of it. I loved it.

***Thanks sooo much Soph, I love it. You're the best :) xxxxx***

My fourteenth birthday was going to be the best birthday yet. This was the new Maddie Beaven. She had not one friend, but two. She was growing into herself at an accelerated rate: she was cool, she was beautiful, and she was just a little bit magic.

Pizza Express was full, but mostly with families and small children and students from the university.

'This is nice, isn't it?' Gran said, squeezing my hand. Usually I might have recoiled from it but today it didn't bother me. 'Fourteen eh? Can't believe it. Where have the years gone? Your Mum would be so proud of you love.'

'Would she?'

'Of course.'

Was this the time to push her on the subject? I decided it wasn't. I was happy, she was happy. Why ruin the moment when I could ask later?

'Anything else for you?', the waitress asked. 'Dessert, coffee?'

'Dessert, please. Banoffee Pie for me. Gran?'

'Oh, that's thrown me. She never has pudding usually', she said, frantically looking at the menu. 'Same for me.'

'I like your hair', said the waitress looking at my perfectly curled pony tail. 'I wish I could do creative things like that with mine. I don't have a clue, anyway it's not thick and shiny like yours.' She sighed, smiling.

'Thanks', I replied, smiling back at her whilst pushing some stray hair behind my ear. Being noticed was something new to me. I used to think that maybe it was a blessing that I was more or less invisible, but I quite liked this new-found attention.

'Pudding and everything, Miss Beaven. What on earth has happened to you?', Gran chuckled.

'It's my birthday, isn't it? I should have asked her to stick a candle in it', I laughed.

'Well, I must say, you seem much more… oh, I don't know, you seem happier', she replied.

'I am.'

'Is it a boy?'

'No! Why would it be a boy? Do you think a boy is the answer, then?', I asked.

I hoped she didn't think Arthur was the answer to her happiness. She definitely didn't need a man for that, she had me.

'No, of course not, silly. I just couldn't think why you're not that anxious little girl anymore. Don't get me wrong, I'm thrilled for you.'

'I've grown into myself at last, Gran', I laughed.

'Yes, you have, love.'

*I will ask her about Mum tomorrow*, I thought.

The afternoon passed without much incident. I sank back onto my pillows and smiled to myself. Today had been a good day so far. I was looking forward to dinner at Cafe Rouge. I would have the duck this time. I always had the chicken usually. *New Maddie has duck*, I thought. Putting on my headphones, I listened to Little Mix until I dozed off into a dreamless sleep.

I was sure my new skirt was excessive for a night out with Gran, but I just couldn't resist wearing it. It fitted perfectly and made my legs look super long and slim. They weren't particularly chunky or anything, but they weren't the best part of me. Not usually, anyway. Tonight - they looked good. I took my hair down and let it fall loosely over my shoulders. I topped up my makeup and even added a bit of eyeliner for good measure. I didn't want to get all big headed or anything and think I was something I wasn't because I might take a tumble amongst all my self-obsessiveness.

God, was that what I had become, self-obsessed? Was liking yourself wrong? Did it make me a bad person? I'd almost become comfortable with my inadequate status. It had become part of who I was and now that person seemed like an imposter. She'd taken over the life I should have been living all this time. For a short moment I felt cross with her.

'Wow, I've not seen you in a skirt for ages, maybe years, even', Gran said as I gripped the hand rail in case I toppled down the stairs in the two-inch heels Sophie had leant me to go with this skirt.

'Is it too much for Cafe Rouge?', I asked.

'Of course not. Why shouldn't you look special on your birthday? You look beautiful, love', she said as she supported me down the last two stairs.

'Thanks.'


Josh! Oh my God, I couldn't believe of all people, he was sitting on the table next to ours. I felt my cheeks burn bright red as I shuffled myself right into the corner of the bench seat and pushed some cushions up against my thigh.

I tried not to look in his direction. I did okay for the first five minutes and then I couldn't help it. It was like something was willing my head to turn and my eyes to look right at him. My head was saying: *what the hell, Maddie?* but somehow, I couldn't help myself.

'Hi', I mouthed as he looked right back at me and smiled. *Oh my God, he smiled back at me.*

'Hi Maddie', he replied. And he actually knew my name, too. Even though I was totally mortified on one hand, I was thrilled on the other. He was with another older boy and people who I supposed were his parents.

'Someone from school?', Gran asked, winking at me and reducing my thrill to embarrassment.

'Yeah, a friend', I answered before she started going on about boyfriends again and thinking I'd arranged for him to be there because we were an item. I wish we were an item... wishful thinking, Maddie.

I told myself that this was one wish that would never come true because some things just can't happen, the natural order of popular versus unpopular would win every time. He'd lose his status as the most popular boy ever in the history of popular boys at St Stephen's and he'd never get it back.

I didn't allow myself to look over again. I told myself that I ought to be grateful for that hi. He'd been kind because he was probably a nice person. He was taking pity on me. That was okay. At least he didn't ignore me and make me feel like an idiot.

I managed to pretend he wasn't there and gave all of my attention to Gran, who must have spent a fortune on me that day. It was then that I decided the time was right to ask.

'Why don't you talk about Mum, Gran?'

'What's to say, love? Some things are best left as they are. No need to stir things up, is there?', she said, which I thought was a bit of a strange thing to say.

'I don't want to talk about the accident or anything', I said. 'I just want to know a bit more about her, that's all. Am I like her?'

'No', she answered, sharply.

'What, not at all?'

'Not really, love. You don't want to compare yourself to your Mum. You're your own person. We don't all take after our parents. I wasn't one bit like my Mother.'

'Why wouldn't I want to be compared to her, though?', I asked, confused. It was like she'd put up some sort of wall and I couldn't break through it. 'There must be something.'

'Not that I can think of', she answered. I knew that was it. There was no way she was going to give me anything. I could only imagine she found it too painful. Mum was her only child so maybe she couldn't bear to talk about her. I was being selfish, and she'd spent all that money on me and given me cash for my skirt. If I wanted to know anything I'd have to try and find it out by other means. I had no idea how to go about it though, because there was no other family I was aware of and I didn't dare push to find out if that was really the case.

# Chapter Six

It was hard to know what to get for someone you didn't really know. I'd asked Gran for ten pounds to put in a card because I didn't want to get something she already had or something she didn't like.

'Wow thanks, Maddie, you didn't have to give me anything', Penny said as she tore open the card. 'That's my food sorted, then!', she laughed.

'That'll just about get you a large popcorn', I laughed back.

There were four other girls there. Trinny Blackwood, Jemma Taylor, Lisa Goodimore and Darcie Woods. Evidently, Darcie had fallen out with Trudy, so Penny hadn't invited her and now they weren't speaking either. *Seriously?* I thought. Five popular girls and me. I felt out of my depth all of a sudden and my momentum felt like it had dipped below what had become normal for me. I took a deep breath and closed my eyes without realising what I was doing.

'Are you okay?', Penny asked full of concern.

'Oh yeah, sorry', I said as I opened my eyes with a start and blushed as I saw everyone looking at me at the same time. I wasn't used to that. It felt like their eyes were burning into me. Like they could see into my soul or something and for a moment I thought they could see I was not like them. I was something different.

I thought, *what if they can tell I did this?* That I cast some sort of spell to be here and they're freaking out. It didn't feel like that's what I had done but, when I came to think about it, that was what I'd done. I was beginning to think it was all in my mind after all or I had actually dropped into some alternate universe where everything was exactly as I'd hoped it would be or that maybe I had died that night in my bed and that this was what heaven was like. It was normal life, only perfect.

'So how long have you two been friends, then?', Darcie asked. God, she thought it was ridiculous, she thought Penny could do better obviously.

'Not long', I replied. I wanted to look at the floor, but I didn't.

'I don't recognise you from school, who's class are you in?'

'Miss Peterson. I don't recognise you either', I lied.

'Oh, I'm in Mrs. Brown's class, god she's such a bitch!', she said. 'Seriously, who is she to say I can't wear open-toed sandals anyway?'

'Oh, bloody hell, I have her for maths. She's a witch', I said. She really was. I didn't get much flack from her, mostly because I never said anything and kept a low profile, but she liked putting people down. I think she was probably bullied when she was young. 'Poor you.'

'Yeah right.' She laughed and linked her arm through mine. I was taken aback but I didn't show it. 'Come on, let's try and get the posh seats. I bet they won't be taken this early.'

We all headed up the stairs and I could feel this massive smile trying to force itself across my face. I successfully managed to control it, though. I didn't want anyone to realise how ecstatic I was. I was out with the popular girls and they didn't think I was a total freak. They seemed to actually like me.


'Maddie?' I felt a hand on my shoulder just as we were queueing up in Costa after the film. 'I thought it was you', Sophie said, throwing her arms around me.

'Oh hi', I said, sheepishly. I hadn't told her I was out with Penny. In fact, I hadn't mentioned Penny since that day in town.

'Where's your Gran?'

'Oh I'm… I'm not here with Gran.'

'Hey Soph!' Penny charged up behind us and linked my arm. Her long fringe flopped into her eyes. She pushed it away and smiled at Sophie 'It's my birthday. We're almost birthday twins, aren't we Mads?', she said, laughing.

'Oh, hi Penny', Sophie replied. She looked at me and I could tell she was hurt. It wasn't fair of her really. Like I said before, she made friends easily. She was easy to like. I, on the other hand, didn't find it easy and I didn't want to feel bad about having friends besides her.

'Did you watch the film too?' Penny asked her.

'No, I'm picking my sister up. She's at a party. They're watching some kids' animation or something', she said, still looking at me.

'Well, it was nice to see you and all that,', Penny said as she collected my frappe from the girl behind the till and handed it to me. 'Come on, Mads, we'll lose our seats in a minute.'

Sophie looked over at the table of cackling girls and back at me. 'Okay, well see you soon then?'

'Yeah sure. I'll text you.' I said. I didn't know what else to say, my mind had gone blank and Penny was shrieking at me so I couldn't concentrate to come up with anything better.

'Right.'

'Yes, what can I get you?' Said the girl impatiently tapping the counter.

'Oh sorry…' Sophie replied.

'Bye then.' I squeezed her arm. 'Speak soon.' I said before I headed towards our table. By the time I sat down and looked over again, she'd gone. I felt sort of bad, but I quashed that feeling. I didn't have to feel bad. I had to start putting me first. Sophie would understand. I'd text her in the morning. I'd invite her over for lunch.


*Dear Diary,*

*Oh my absolute God! I have had the best day ever. I have six friends now, if I include Sophie. Is there anything I can't make happen? It seems the happier I am, the more good things happen. Perhaps that's the secret to this spell. I have to stay happy and then all things are possible.*

*Sophie was cross with me. I could tell she was. She'll get over it, though. She's just not used to seeing me with anyone else. Maybe she was jealous. I can't let her feelings cloud mine. I am number one and I am loving this new me. I've almost forgotten the old Maddie. God, she was such a loser.*

## Chapter Seven

I was pretty sure Gran was on a date. *Who was she kidding saying he was just a friend?* Would you buy a new dress to go out with a friend? No, of course not.

I didn't know how I felt about it. I think I was annoyed or irritated or maybe even a bit jealous. I was terrified of letting that emotion get to me and take hold because then I might lose everything. I really can't stress strongly enough how much I didn't want Gran to have a man. I had convinced myself that it was okay for things to be about me and how I felt, it was okay to de-wish him. I was sure I could just as easily evaporate him. She'd realise that he wasn't right for her and that would be that.

I'd see what happened after tonight. I probably wouldn't even need to put the wish into my box because she would probably have a horrible time and I wouldn't have to be the one to put a stop to it. I wasn't being unreasonable. I was being practical. We didn't have room in the house for a man. The cottage was small, even for both of us. I just wished the niggling little thing inside of me would shut up. If I had been given all this power, then why I being allowed to doubt myself? Was it a test or something? What was I supposed to do?

I'd decided to forget about it for now. I had more pressing matters to deal with. I had decided that a wish for Josh was okay. I mean, I was verging on popular myself, now. Penny was texting me all the time and even Darcie texted me yesterday. I decided to get Facebook. Penny said it was naff and that everyone our age has SnapChat now, but I didn't understand it. Facebook seemed pretty simple and it was a start. Even though no-one used it much, I knew that Josh had it. I checked. So, I might need to have it in order for him to ask me out. I was almost convinced this would happen now. It was like my momentum had had a boost overnight or something. I thought that maybe all the good stuff super charged it. So, I couldn't let the Gran situation get to me. It would all work out right for me. I just had to believe in magic, that was all.

It was five past ten and Gran still wasn't back. I was busying myself making a pot of tea and getting some crumpets out ready to toast for us when she came in. I was sure she'd be all disappointed and regret spending all of that money on a dress for nothing. Ten past, twenty past… still she wasn't back. I could feel anxiety creeping in, trying to force my momentum out so it could take over. I couldn't let that happen, not under any circumstances. If she wasn't back by half-past then I'd call the police because he might have attacked her or have her tied up somewhere because he was actually a psychopath. I wouldn't have been at all surprised. He didn't even come in and say hello when he picked her up. *How rude*, I thought. I had already decided I didn't like him and I couldn't think how anything could change my mind.

Half past ten on the dot, I heard her key in the door. Actually, I'd seen them pulling up. I was tempted to tell her off: *How dare you come back at this hour, young lady?* or something like that. It wasn't all that late, really. It was just that I'd been thinking she'd be home earlier because I was here all alone and I was still only fourteen after all. It might even be illegal to leave me alone all this time, I thought.

'Hi', I said, as casually as I could. 'Did you have a nice time?'

I fully expected her usual sigh, followed by a fall onto the sofa in relief.

'Yes, thanks love', she said. 'Really nice. I don't think I've ever been so full up in my entire life. I feel I could pop at any minute.'

'Oh. So, you like him?', I asked incredulously. 'He didn't even come in and say hello to me.'

'No, but that wasn't down to him. I told him not to, I didn't want you to get all funny with him. Sorry love, did you want to meet him then?'

'Funny with him? Why would I be funny with him?', I asked defensively.

'Well you've been a bit funny about it, haven't you? And I told you he was just a friend.'

'No, I haven't. I've been very good about it, actually. Even though his wife has only just died and everything.'

'She's been dead two years, Maddie. Don't you want me to have a friend, then? You have them, why shouldn't I?'

God, I felt like a complete bitch all of a sudden. Just because I wanted him gone, it didn't mean I had to make it so obvious. I mean, I could get rid of him at the drop of a hat anyway. I didn't have to be so horrible to Gran. I'd make my wish before I went to bed and then I'd let my magic get to work. She'd be fine. Like I said, we didn't have room for a man and even though she said he was just a friend, I felt deep down that he might be more some-day and I didn't want him to be. Gran could get a man when I was off at university or college or wherever I went when I'd finished my exams. I thought she was being a bit selfish to be honest.

*I wish Arthur would go away*

There, that was easy. Now all I had to do was wait for him to disappear. I had no idea how he might 'go away' but I didn't doubt that he would. I pushed the seed of doubt away that entered my head. Not the doubt that he would indeed disappear but doubt that it was the right thing to do.

'Maddie, Sophie's on the phone, love.' Gran called up to me. Shit, I'd forgotten all about her. I'd promised to text her, but I hadn't.

'Okay.' I called back. I'd have to make something up. I'd say I'd had a migraine or something. 'Coming.'

'Hi.'

'Alright. You didn't text me. What have you been up to?'

'Nothing much. I don't always have to text you first do I?', I said, irritated. Why was it always me? She could just have easily have texted me.

'Course not. It's just that you said you would and well… I was worried that's all.'

'You don't have to be. I'm fine.'

'Okay, so shall we do something today then? Mum's working but Tiegen is at Aunty Jackie's so I've got all day if you want to go into town or something.'

I had plans to see Darcie and Penny. We were going into town because Penny had almost fifty pounds birthday money to spend. I had about three pounds in my piggy bank. Enough to get me a Happy Meal.

'Can't today.'

I did consider telling her. I really did, but when it came to it, I lied.

'I promised to help Gran with the shopping because she's hurt her arm.' Shit, what an absolute and total lie. I didn't even know where it came from. 'Sorry, maybe tomorrow?'

'That's a shame', she said, disappointed. 'It can't be helped. No worries. Yeah, I could probably do the afternoon tomorrow, any good?'

I couldn't very well say no because I won't have any money by then, so I said okay. I felt horrible, actually. I tried to convince myself that I was being kind, but that wasn't kind. *Why didn't I ask her to join us?* I knew Penny wouldn't have minded and I was pretty sure Darcie wouldn't either. Penny liked Sophie and Darcie would have too once she got to know her. The thing was, I didn't want her to be there. She might have pinched them from me without even realising. They might like her better and forget all about me. It wasn't as if I even knew how this magic thing really worked. I wasn't sure how long I had it and I was starting to worry that it was slipping away from me already.

I slipped on a short, black, backless dress with my baseball boots. I'd never worn it before because I felt it was too clingy and I thought my legs were too big for it.

*I can't think why I haven't worn this before*, I said to myself as I admired my slim figure in the full-length mirror. I'd pretty much forgotten about the Sophie incident. I grabbed my loose change and headed off with excitement. I had great hopes for what the day might bring.


'Maddie!' They both shrieked as I confidently walked over to my new-found friends. 'Love that dress', said Darcie.

'Me too', said Penny. 'God my legs would look crap in a dress like that.'

'What? But you've got great legs', I replied.

'No way, they're all out of proportion with the rest of me… look!', she said as she grabbed her tiny waist with both hands. 'Fat arse and minuscule waist. Ridiculous. God knows how I'm going to find anything decent to wear. I never can, usually.'

I'd assumed everyone except me was super confident in themselves, but it seemed like everyone had their own hang ups. Maybe I wasn't that different. Maybe the old Maddie was more normal than I'd given her credit for.

We ambled around the shops for a couple of hours. Penny tried on numerous dresses and jeans but ended up with three t-shirts from H&M.

'I told you I wouldn't find anything', she laughed. 'I'm crap at shopping. I need someone to do it for me, like a personal shopper.'

'You always look lovely', I said. She did, I couldn't really see what she was complaining about to be honest.

'Hey, isn't that your friend over there, Maddie?', said Darcie.

I looked in the direction she was pointing with dread filling the whole of me and completely overwhelming my momentum. It took over just like that. I hoped she hadn't seen me, but I knew she had. I just stood there staring at her as she looked at me and then turned and walked towards the bus stop without even saying hello.

'You two fallen out or something?', Penny asked.

'Not really. I don't think so anyway. I didn't tell her I was coming with you guys today.'

'So?', Darcie said, pulling her shoulder length hair into a bun at the back of her head, 'You can have more than one friend, you know. God is she all possessive and that? I hate girls like that.'

'No, no not at all. Sophie isn't like that. She's… I should have invited her, that's all…'. I trailed off. I felt awful. All I wanted to do was go home and hide under my duvet. I didn't even know if she'd ever speak to me again. I didn't want to text or call her. I was too cowardly.

For the next four or five days, I obsessed over a text or a call. *Would she ever call me again?* I didn't even want to see anyone else, not even Penny. Why did I think it was okay to do that? Sophie had been there for me always and I just dropped her from a great height for two people I hardly knew.

It wasn't even that it was their fault. They wouldn't have cared if I'd invited Sophie along. This was all down to me and my obsession with being popular. I didn't even care about it anymore. *So what if no-one got me?* I was probably fine just the way I was. I doubted any of this new stuff was magic after all. I'd just believed that it was. I'd made things happen just because I thought something else was in control and had given me some sort of special power or something.

It all seemed so stupid in that moment. Who was I kidding? Magic didn't exist, of course it didn't. If I really could do magic, then this wouldn't have happened. I'd tried for days to get Sophie to text me. I'd put it into my wish box, not once but three times and still nothing. It seemed like the more I wished for it, the further and further away it got.

## Chapter Eight

'Oh love, just call her. Sophie's a level-headed sort. She'll understand if you explain and apologise', Gran said when I refused my toast and tea that morning. 'You can't stop eating.'

'Why would she understand? I wouldn't', I said, with tears welling up in my eyes.

'Well one thing's for sure, love, you won't know that if you don't at least give her the chance.'

She was right, I knew she was. I was scared but, not only that, I didn't want to beg. I knew I was in the wrong, but I couldn't bear to reduce myself to that. Maybe my wish would just take a while longer this time. I would just keep trying. I wasn't ready to give up on this magic thing quite yet. Even though I thought I'd probably gone mad or something, I still couldn't quite let it go. Perhaps it was desperation.

A few days later, after it had become obvious that Sophie wasn't going to make first contact, I decided to open that Facebook account. Maybe she'd send me a friend request or something and we'd be alright again. I mean, maybe I was over-thinking the whole thing. Perhaps she really wasn't upset at all and I was just making this whole scenario up and wasting my energy.

Anyway, whatever the case was, I had to keep occupied. I was going mad and I felt crap all the time. My momentum had depleted to almost nothing and I guessed that was why nothing was happening for me; that and the fact that I'd pretty much stayed in bed for the past few days. It was still there though, in the background. Even after all this, it hadn't given up on me. I woke up last night and had this overwhelming feeling that I just had to stop wanting her to contact me and get on with my life. I had come this far. Was I really going to go back to the way I was? I didn't think I could bear it. I should have done the noble thing and contacted her. *Why was I being so bloody stubborn?* I sort of knew she'd forgive me because that was the sort of person she was. She didn't bear a grudge. I don't think she knew how to even if she'd wanted to. But I wanted to keep the control, I suppose.

I didn't dare admit that to myself but deep down I knew that's what it was. I was popular Maddie now, with friends in high places and a potential gorgeous boyfriend. If I went back to her all grovelly and *oh please forgive me I'm so terrible, I don't deserve you then I might as well just give up this new me, the magic me,* I reasoned. One more shove and I just knew it would be gone. It was there, just. I had to get back control. What would have been the point of it all if I just gave in to other people's desires instead of getting what was rightfully mine?

Even before I'd added a few carefully selected selfies, there it was. A little red spot on the two people at the top of the page. I'd assumed it was some sort of automated thing but to my delight, it was a request from him… Josh! Within a few seconds, my magic momentum had soared. It was swishing around inside of me and I felt like nothing in the world could ever get the better of me, not ever.

*I am magic, I am magic,* I said to myself over and over. What did this mean? Even if he just wanted to be my friend and had no ideas about anything else, it didn't matter because I was Facebook friends with Josh Howells. I had finally made it and it hadn't even been hard work. I started thinking about all of the things I could achieve. I mean, if I'd achieved this absolutely impossible thing then I could achieve anything I wanted.

Something was trying to talk to me, though. It wasn't a strong voice or anything, but it was there in the background telling me that this was all too good to be true and who did I think I was anyway?

*'Hey Maddie, fancy coming over to mine? My Mum's at work until 7 and we've got pizza! ;) ;) ;) xxx*

Penny was fast becoming my Sophie substitute. If Sophie wasn't going to call or friend request me then that was up to her. I had friends now. Ones that did want to friend me and now I had SnapChat. Josh had liked all of my photos on Facebook and even waved at me. I went red, even though there was nobody else there.

I did miss Sophie, but I was trying really hard not to. When I thought about her, I just got all knotted up inside and it wasn't good for me. It made me feel uneasy and I didn't like the feeling. Maybe I was moving on. Perhaps this was just the natural order of things. She was my everything because I didn't have the luxury of choice. Now it was like nobody even knew I was anything other than this person. It wasn't the easiest transition, if I'm being completely honest. There were times when I longed for a day alone to trawl through Google looking at articles on quantum physics, but that Maddie was gone. I trampled all of the old traits down into the depths of me. I couldn't rid myself of them completely and sometimes I felt them pushing to get out. I had to take a few deep breaths and remind myself that this was better. What I had now was everything. I'd get over all that geeky stuff in time. I just had to ignore it a while longer until it became unnatural to me.

I had to take a bus to Penny's because it was a good thirty-minute walk and I didn't much like physical exercise. The weather hadn't changed much in three weeks. The sun was still shining, and it was super-hot. Much hotter than it had been in August, ever in the history of recorded Augusts so they'd said on the news last night. I was just pulling my hair up into a messy bun like I'd learnt to do recently when I saw her. Sophie was getting onto the bus. Tiegan was yanking at her hand as she was trying to pay. She didn't yell at her or get impatient like I would have done.

'Just find a seat, I'll be there in a minute', she said as her unruly little sister ran to the back right towards me. Oh God, this was going to be awkward...

'Oh hi', Sophie said as she moved Tiegen into the window seat and sat next to me.

'How are you?', she asked. If she felt awkward, she didn't show it.

'Okay… fine, yeah I'm doing good thanks', I replied. I wanted the floor of the bus to open up and for me to fall out onto the hard concrete so that it might knock some sense into me. What I actually wanted to say was *I'm not doing too bad, but I miss you. I'm sorry.*

'Good. I've got her for the day', she said, gesturing at Tiegan, who was licking the window like an excitable dog. 'Don't do that', she said, before sighing to me, 'She'll do what she wants, as usual.' She sighed again as Tiegen continued to do more of the same.

It's hard to explain how I was feeling as we sat in relative silence until she got off at the stop opposite the park. 'See you around, then', she said.

'Yeah… yeah course, see you at school then', I said pathetically. I was compelled to run after her. Something told me to get off that bloody bus right there and then, but I ignored it. The compulsion to follow her was intense. It almost overwhelmed me. Why didn't I do it? It wasn't even as if I didn't think it was the right thing to do or that I was better off not having her in my life. But something inside of me refused to budge.

What was the point having all this magic if I couldn't use if for the stuff I really wanted? How had I managed to get all these other cool things to happen just by putting wishes into the box, yet I couldn't get my best friend of all time back? How could something so simple be so difficult? If only I'd been a grown up and just said I was sorry. I was trying so hard to make magic do it for me that I'd lost sight of the fact that all I really had to do was swallow my pride.

## Chapter Nine

I really did like Penny. She was fun, and she liked me. Well, she liked this Maddie. I wasn't so sure how she'd feel about geek Maddie. I wasn't going to take a chance on finding out.

Over the last few weeks of the holidays, we saw lots of each other. Sometimes with Darcie and sometimes with the others, too. There was nothing wrong with my new life. There were parts of it I adored. Mostly the part where Josh had become my boyfriend. Me, Maddie Beaven, had an actual real-life boyfriend, and not one that Gran had set me up with. It had happened so seamlessly, I almost forgot the point where we changed from friends to something else. He was nice. Way nicer than I thought it was possible for popular boys to be. I had had this grossly skewed notion that anyone popular was actually not very nice, or that they had some other vice or issue because nobody could be popular and nice both at the same time. I was one of them now. I was one of the it-crowd. We were back at school, in year ten, almost adults.

I'd started working in the kitchen at the King's Head. Just washing plates and clearing tables. Nothing glamorous, but I got almost five pounds an hour and with my first pay packet I bought two new pairs of lacy knickers from Beau Avenue. Penny came with me. 'Ask that girl to help you', she said, pointing at one of the sales assistants before looking in the mirror, trying unsuccessfully to tuck her growing out fringe behind her left ear. Then she just wandered off. 'I'm gonna look at the pyjamas, catch up with you in a bit', she called back. I felt a bit lost for a moment, I longed for Sophie. She would have helped me choose.

I'd see Sophie around school. We always said hi and sometimes she'd ask about Gran. I got a tug in my stomach every time she stopped to chat and, secretly, I longed to tell her how I really felt but I thought she'd probably moved on. It was never for long, and it was not as awkward as it used to be. She got about with Sammy Newport, who she met at netball.

'Is Arthur coming over tonight?', I asked Gran as she stirred the gravy. 'I haven't seen him in ages', I said as I realised he hadn't been over in a while, at least a couple of weeks.

'I think he's dumped me. That's what you young one's say isn't it?', she replied, laughing even though I could see she was hurt. 'I think he got scared, love. Men are like that, aren't they? Can't handle their emotions, that's what my Mother used to say.'

'Oh no. Has he said anything?'

'Nope. Just ignores me like I don't exist. Oh well, his loss.'

I stopped in my tracks. I'd wished him gone. Had I done this? Surely it wasn't possible. I'd pretty much forgotten about magic. It seemed childish and I had started to think I'd made it all up in my head because things don't just magic themselves into existence and I am not some sort of white witch, of course I'm not. I'll be fifteen in a few months. I'd grown out of all that nonsense. Still, I couldn't put it out of my mind. Why would he just stop talking to her? They were great together. I'd come to like him, actually. He made Gran happy and who was I to say she couldn't have a man in her life?

I'd forgotten about Mum. I was going to try and find out about her. I'd made it a mission but then my life had changed so dramatically, so quickly that it didn't seem important.

I didn't know why it suddenly seemed important again, but it did. I hadn't had that feeling in a while. The one I used to refer to as momentum. When I thought about all that stuff, I felt stupid. I actually believed in magic, like it was absolutely possible that I could change my life just by believing in it and asking for stuff. At that moment, I felt the rush again. It felt like an old friend, familiar and comforting. I felt it as I thought about her.

As quickly as the feeling came, it left me. I stuffed some cheese burger into my mouth as Josh put his arm over my shoulder and planted a wet kiss on my cheek. 'I'm eating, get off.' It all came out garbled and he laughed.

'What was that, Beaven?', he said, still laughing at me. 'Did you say something?', he said as he kissed me again.

'Come on, you two!' Penny shrieked.

'We'll miss the bus in a minute!', shouted Darcie.

I looked around at my friends. How had this happened? I barely remembered. For a split second I thought about Sophie. I wondered how I'd let our friendship go. She could be here now, laughing along with all of us. It wasn't as if I didn't like my new friends just as much as I liked Sophie. It was just that we had something special, Sophie and me. I'd come to realise that that sort of connection with another person is rare.

'You okay?', Josh asked as he waved his hand in front of my face. 'What are you thinking about?'

'Oh nothing, just daydreaming.' I replied as I got up and stuffed my rubbish into the bin.

As I lay in bed that night, I couldn't sleep. Usually I'd be out like a light as soon as my head hit the pillow. That night my head felt like it was filled with a mass of tangled wires, all joining up and making wrong connections. I didn't feel like me. I sat up with my heart pounding and my hair wet with sweat. I had no idea where all this had come from. I had been fine when I'd got into bed. I did have Gran on my mind, and Mum, I suppose, but I wasn't stressed or anxious or anything. Now I felt both. I felt like I needed a little man to get inside of my head and unpick all of the wires and match them with the right connections. Who was I?

I was pretending to be one thing when, really, I was another. Was I just having some sort of episode and everything would be okay when I woke up? Gran would say it was my hormones rushing all over the place, probably, but it wasn't that. I felt like I was losing my mind. Shit, there was no pleasing me. I'd wanted all of this. I'd forgotten that I'd dreamt about this life, that I'd imagined having all of this. The thing I wanted more than anything, though, was to have Sophie back. I'd not so much pushed the thought away until now but sat on it. She was always there though. Even when I was with Josh or hanging out with the girls, she was never far from my thoughts. It wasn't like I ever sat down and analysed my feelings or anything, more that I felt her, if that makes sense. Probably not. I'd had the chance that day on the bus. It was almost as if the universe gave it to me and I blew it by being all stubborn and proud.

My eyes started to feel heavy. I could feel my body releasing the tension that was stored up inside of it, pushing at my skin to get out. The feelings were slowly evaporating, and I was beginning to feel normal again. *I suppose these things happen in the middle of the night*, I thought. My brain was all tired and didn't want to be awake, so it started acting up to freak me out. Like a small child having a tantrum.

'Why don't you call Arthur, Gran?', I asked as I poured us both some tea. 'He might be ill or something.'

'Really?' She replied. 'I hadn't thought about that. No, this all happened when I mentioned making this thing official.'

'What do you mean official? Like marriage?'

'God no. I said perhaps he might move in or at least stay over sometimes.'

'And he didn't want to?'

'Who knows, love? He went quiet and I haven't heard from him since', she said. 'Stands to reason he's got cold feet. I expect he just wanted a bit of fun, that's all.'

'I don't know…', I said, stirring sugar into my tea. 'He seemed pretty keen to me.'

'And to me, but you just don't know what's going on in a person's head, do you?'

She was right there, I supposed. I was a prime example of that. But Arthur seemed to genuinely love her. My wish popped into my mind again. I cursed myself for being so childish, now and then. *Of course you did not wish Arthur away*, I told myself. *Don't be so thirteenish*. I'd changed so much since then. I wasn't sure I wanted him to move in permanently, but it wasn't my choice to make.

'Go and see him', I said but she shook her head violently.

'Absolutely not. He's made his choice. I'm not about to start begging', she said determinedly. How could I argue against that? After all, that's exactly what I'd done with Sophie.

'Don't be stubborn, Gran. You might regret it.'

'No, it's done love. Over and done with and now I don't want to talk about it, okay?' She meant it. I could tell she was as determined not to contact him as I had been not to contact Sophie.

*I wish Arthur would come back.*

Could I really be so ridiculous as to think a wish would make any difference? I felt like an idiot when I popped it into the box. Well, one thing was for sure, it wasn't going to hurt to ask. It wasn't like anyone knew about my wish box. In a while I'd smash it up and be done with all that nonsense once and for all.

# Chapter Ten

'Madilyn, isn't it?', she asked. 'Louise's grand-daughter?' She was old, not old like Gran but old.

'Maddie, yeah' No-one called me Madilyn. I forgot it was my actual name and it didn't feel right.

'Sorry, do I know you?'

I also forgot Gran had a name other than Gran.

'No, you don't, not personally. I'm Sarah. I know your Gran… knew her, I guess.' She trailed off. 'I've seen pictures. She sends me one now and again. I've got a couple of school photos of you and a lovely one from Christmas last year.'

She was looking at me intently. Like she was studying every little freckle and imperfection.

'Fancy seeing you like this. I recognised you right away, even though you look a bit older now.'

'Why do you have photos of me?', I asked, confused.

'Hasn't Louise mentioned me then?', she asked.

'No, no she hasn't.'

'I was a friend of your Mum. Me and Emma were inseparable. All the way until… well.'

'Until she died?' I said.

'Um… yes.'

'I don't know much about her, really. Gran doesn't talk about her. Too upsetting for her I suppose', I said. 'Can you tell me about her?'

'What do you want to know?'. She started rummaging through her bag. 'It's probably not the best time to be honest, actually I'm running late for something.'

'You don't live around here, do you?', I asked. 'Otherwise we'd have met before.'

'Cardiff. I'm just visiting…'

'Have you got time for a coffee?', I asked. 'There's a new Starbucks on the High Street.' I didn't feel right about letting her go. I felt I'd probably never see her again and I'd be left with questions I'd never find answers for. I didn't know what it was, but I just knew I had to talk to her. If nothing else, she'd known Mum and I could ask her what she was really like.

'I really can't right now Maddie. Look, let me have your number and I'll try and see you before I go', she said as she pulled her phone from her bag. 'Add it for me will you. I can't get my head around this techy stuff', she said as if mobile phones were all new to her.

I added my number to her contacts. 'Don't you have WhatsApp?'

'I have no idea what that is, Maddie love', she laughed. 'As you can probably tell, I don't do technology. Well not very well anyway.'

'Have you seen Gran then?'

'I was planning to but not yet. Is she well?', she asked.

'Yeah, she's okay. Do you know someone else here then?' I continued to push her. 'If you're not from here have you come to see someone?'

'Well coincidentally I'm here to pick up a three-piece suite I won on eBay. Just the right colours and only a hundred quid. Looks brand new in the pictures. Worth the drive for that sort of a saving. Hubby is here, too. He's the one with the van. Funny that, isn't it? Never thought I'd see your Gran after she moved. She's never been one for much contact, what with her not driving and everything. I did call her to say I was coming but she didn't answer.' Gran didn't tell me she'd lived in Cardiff. I always just assumed I was from Caltherton.

'So, Mum was from Cardiff then?' I asked.

'Blimey, your Gran really hasn't told you much, has she?' She said raising her eyebrows and creasing up her forehead.

'No, not really.' I mean, it's not like it matters or anything but it might have been nice to know I was born in Cardiff. Sort of seems like the kind of thing I should know.

'Well I'll call you. I'm here until Thursday. It's just, well, I feel like I ought to speak to Louise first. You know what I mean?'

I didn't want her to. I felt there was something I didn't know. Not just the little things but something big and I didn't want Gran telling her not to see me.

'She's not here', I blurted out. 'She's away for a couple of days. In Cornwall', I lied some more.

'Oh well, that's why she didn't get back to me then. Does she have a mobile phone?'

'No.' She did. One of those stupid huge ones with the massive numbers for people who can't see very well, even though she doesn't even need glasses. I was always embarrassed when she took it out in public.

'Right, well, never mind. It would have been nice to catch up with her, but it can't be helped. Oh well, I'll call you this evening probably then. Perhaps we can meet up tomorrow before I leave. You will be okay, won't you? Talking about her will be okay for you? I mean, it's a difficult thing to talk about your Mum and not talk about what happened.'

'I'll be okay yes thanks.' I didn't know if I would be okay, but I wasn't going to say as much. This was my chance. What were the chances of this really? It was like...... *don't be stupid, Maddie.* I berated myself.

# Chapter Eleven

I'm not sure I'd ever been so nervous about anything in my life. How silly, I thought. It was just that talking to someone, I mean really talking to someone about Mum. It made her real. Before she'd been this... oh I don't know, this enigma, I suppose. It was like she was a fairytale princess or something.

'What would you like to know then, Maddie?', Sarah said, passing me the sugar. 'We were like sisters, you know?', she said with her hand cupping mine.

'Like... what was she like? I mean, was she funny, was she shy, was she confident...?'

'Your Mum was a complete and utter contradiction', she said, smiling. 'She could be full of confidence one day and then shy as you like the very next. She was into the stars, you know, astrology.'

'Astronomy', I corrected her.

'Yes, of course, astrology is something completely different isn't it?' She laughed out loud. 'I've never been very good with words. I always mix things up.'

I liked Sarah. She was sweet, and she seemed kind. She was one of those people you just took to for no explainable reason. She had this mass of curly blond hair. It was a mess really, but it seemed to suit her.

'I'm into that stuff. Well, I was', I said, ashamed of the fact that I'd tried not to be.

'Are you? Oh, that's wonderful. It's lovely to know she's passed something on to you, just lovely.'

'Was she clever?'

'Not in the conventional sense of the word, but she was bright. She didn't like school one bit. I don't know why, really, because she had lots of friends and she got by, you know? I loved school. Everything was simple then.'

'How old was she, when she died I mean?'

'Twenty-three. I'll never forget the day it happened. The worst day of my life so far it was. No signs at all. I still don't understand it really. She had her moments, of course, but to do that. I suppose if you've never felt like that then you just can never really understand, can you?'

I knew that she wasn't referring to an accident. I had a sick feeling in the pit of my stomach. Gran had lied to me all these years. How could she do that to me? 'She killed herself?'

'Well, yes. But you knew that, right?' Sarah looked concerned, mortified in fact. I felt bad for deceiving her. 'You did know that didn't you, Maddie?'

'I'd like to lie to you, Sarah, because I know it would make you feel better, but I just can't. No, I didn't know. Gran said she'd died in a car crash, but I never really thought it was true. No, more like I thought she was leaving something out.'

'Oh Maddie, Is your Gran really away?'

'No, sorry', I said sheepishly. 'I just didn't want her to stop you from seeing me. Why do you think she lied?'

'You shouldn't have lied to me, Maddie. I feel terrible', she said. 'Anyway, I can only imagine she didn't want you to know the truth because it's so awful. A car crash would have been out of Emma's control. Suicide is a choice and she had you so…'

'I suppose. How could she do that?' I could feel tears pricking my eyes. I was trying so hard

not to let any fall. 'How could any mother?'

'Who knows, Maddie? All I can say is that she loved you. Really, really loved you. She could have given you up or had an abortion, but she wouldn't hear of it, even when that coward did a runner.'

'My Dad?' I asked. I'd never even thought about him. I'd always assumed he wasn't around anyway. 'Who was he?'

'Adam Matthews. He was alright, as it goes. Well, I thought he was. They were going to get married. We were looking at dresses and everything. I was going to be bridesmaid. I was so excited. That was all after she'd told him too. He seemed okay about it, quite supportive actually. Then he just buggers off without a word. Off travelling around Australia, he'd said when he'd emailed her. He was a couple of years younger than her, so I suppose he just got cold feet and well, she could be hard work. Clearly it was more than that, but she never confided. Not in me, not in anyone. I wish I'd noticed. How could I not have noticed?'

'I feel sick.' I said as I put my hand over my mouth.

'Oh darling', she said, putting her arm around me and pulling me into her waist. 'I'm so sorry. I'd never have told you if your Gran had asked me not to. She never once said anything. It didn't cross my mind that she may not have told you the truth. I hope you won't let this cloud your view of your Mum. She was the loveliest girl, you know? I miss her terribly, still. I've never had a friend like her since.'

I felt awful for putting her in that position, but I had to know. Now I felt like screaming at the top of my lungs. I was so mad at Gran for lying to me. How dare she decide that I shouldn't know the truth?

'Is it true?' I shouted so loud my voice cracked. 'Don't lie to me again!' I didn't know why I was asking. It was true, of course it was.

'What on earth is it, love?', she said, holding my right arm.

*How dare she? How dare she lie to me all this time? I hate her, I hate her, I hate her.*

'Is it true that Mum topped herself?' I screamed with tears rolling down my cheeks and into my mouth. I hate that term, I didn't know why I'd used it. It was such a flippant way to describe something so awful.

'Who on earth… how?', she stuttered.

'Sarah, her friend Sarah. You know, the one you avoided when she called'

'Sarah?'

'Sarah, yes!', I shrieked some more. 'How could you not tell me something like that?'

'Oh, Maddie', she said as she tried to wrap both arms around my waist. 'I'm so very sorry, love…'

'You're just sorry I found out, that's all. You should have told me!' By now, tears were uncontrollably running down my cheeks, making a mess of my white shirt. 'I can never trust a word you say ever again.' I shrieked again as I slammed the living room door and ran up to my room.


'Love… Maddie, love. Open the door. This won't solve anything, will it?', she said tapping lightly on my bedroom door. 'Come on, let me in love.'

'Go away!', I yelled. 'Just go away and leave me alone.'

'Maddie', she said with a cracked voice. So, she was upset, so what?

'Please go away, Gran. I can't talk to you right now.'

'Okay love. We'll talk tomorrow, then.' I heard her walk along the landing and back down the stairs. I wasn't sure I'd ever want to talk to her again.

## Chapter Twelve

I didn't know what time it was. My phone was dead and I couldn't be bothered to get up and charge it. I could hear Gran downstairs. Why hadn't she come up to see how I was? I was distraught last night, I thought. I might have done something stupid like Mum, but she wouldn't know because she can't be arsed to come up here and check on me.

The longer I laid there, the more frustrated and irritable I started to become. I'd just found out my Mum had taken her own life. That wasn't a small thing, it was a huge thing, a ginormous thing. It was like she didn't care that I was beside myself, either that or she'd decided to bury her head in the sand like she had been doing all these years and act as if nothing had happened. Maybe she'd refuse to even tell me why she'd kept it from me or, worse still, just ignore me when I tried to talk to her. While I thought all of this, I knew deep down I was wrong. I was just so cross with her, I wanted to think the absolute worst of her no matter what I knew to be the case. I could hear her cooking bacon or something.

*So, she thinks she can win me over with that, does she?* I said to myself, even more annoyed than I had been five minutes before.

What I really felt, and I couldn't admit to myself, was anger at Mum. She had a baby: me. She'd rather have left me to fend for myself than stay and look after me, or at the very least make sure I was okay before she did it. I didn't even know how she did it. I forgot to ask. I was so shocked at Sarah's revelation that I had completely forgotten to find out how she died.

Was I so unimportant to her? Sarah said she really loved me but how could she have? I couldn't understand her. I had tried last night. I'd thought about the terrible state she must have been in to do something like that and tried to empathise with her, but I just couldn't. I even found myself getting mad at Sarah for not knowing what sort of a mess her best friend was in. I'd have known, for sure I would have known. If it was Sophie I'd have known.

Deep down, Sophie was still my best friend. I had never quite let go of her. I knew she'd moved on and she was probably better off without me in her life, but I still had regret. And hope, I suppose.

Was there anything worse than hope? At some point you're going to be disappointed. Hope leads to more hope, and more, until you finally realise it's never going to happen, and you've wasted way too much of your short life thinking it might. My thoughts turned to magic again. I felt exasperated with myself that I couldn't let go of this notion that if I only could do it right, make the wish in the right way, then she'd come back. How could there be a wrong way? A wish was just a wish wasn't it?

After what seemed like forever, Gran tapped my door. 'Maddie love, I've made breakfast. Bacon and eggs and fried bread, the lot. You going to come down?', she asked.

'Maybe', I answered. 'In a bit.' I was starving. The thought of a cooked breakfast was making my stomach gurgle. I didn't want to go down there too readily or she would think it was all okay and *how dare she think she could bribe me into understanding with a cooked breakfast?*

'Morning', she said as I plonked myself down opposite her. 'Now I know we need to talk Maddie, but we'll do it after we've eaten, okay?', she said.

'Whatever', I replied as I dunked my knife in the butter and spread a thick layer all over a piece of toast. 'Fried bread and toast? Not sure I can eat both', I said. I could quite easily have eaten both.

'Doesn't matter. Just eat what you can, love', she said. 'Are you seeing the girls today?'

It was Saturday. I always saw them on Saturday mornings. Friends in the morning and Josh in the afternoon after he'd finished at football. Then off to work at four. I didn't feel like doing any of that today. I wanted to stay cocooned in my duvet until next weekend.

'Dunno. Don't feel like it to be honest. You do know that I'm devastated, don't you?' I glared at her. She didn't seem to be taking this at all seriously. It was like she thought we'd have our little chat and everything would be okay. 'This is huge, Gran.'

'Yes, I know it is and I'm truly sorry. Eat up and then you can go and get yourself ready. We'll talk when you're all sorted', she said, clearing my plate before I'd even attempted to eat the fried bread. I felt cross with myself for saying I couldn't eat it now. I didn't know where my appetite had come from. It seemed wrong to want to eat somehow. It was like I was being disrespectful to Mum or something, now I knew the truth.

Even though I felt rubbish, I decided that was no good reason not to make an effort. I put on my favourite jeans and my cropped jumper. There was no reason to go to hell just because I knew this. Nothing had changed. I was still the same Maddie, everything was the same only it wasn't somehow. Saying my Mum had died in a car crash was somehow way more acceptable than saying she'd killed herself. I didn't think I'd ever admit it to another soul for as long as I lived. I decided that, after today, I would put it away in my head somewhere. Never think about it again just in case it brought something out in me. I mean what if I took after her and it was in me all just waiting to come out?

'Well?', I said as I deployed myself onto the sofa with extra force.

'Well, where do I start?', she said. 'At the beginning I suppose.'

'That might be a good place, yeah', I replied, sarcastically.

'She was a good girl, always said please and thank you and always ate her meals up. Did as she was told really, not all of the time but most of it', she said, leaning back next to me. 'Anxious little thing, though. Low self-esteem I suppose they'd say now. It was more than that though. It was as if she was forever unsettled. Like something was missing, you see.' She looked at me. 'Bit like you were.'

'It wasn't like that. I wasn't like her', I said defensively. 'I was just weird', I said. 'I'm okay now.'

'You weren't weird, Madilyn. You were a normal pre-adolescent girl. A bit nervy and a bit awkward but never weird.' She said smiling at me. 'What is weird anyway?'

'So yeah, carry on.'

'Well, she started to get these panic attacks. Not many but maybe one a month perhaps. Nothing too worrying, people get them, they are common. But one day, just after an episode she looked right at me and she said What is the point of me? And she really was serious. I had this feeling deep down that it might be more than a bit of anxiety. Your Grandad said I was being silly because she was fifteen at the time and he said what fifteen-year old doesn't have a few issues? Well, I thought he was probably right and thought no more about it. I mean, she quickly took it back after she'd said it, so I thought that perhaps she was acting up you know, like teenagers do sometimes? She wasn't prone to that though. Are you okay for me to go on?', she asked.

'Course', I said. I was transfixed. I knew this story did not have a happy ending but all the same. 'Go on.'

'Well she never said another thing about it, or like it. Not until she was with Adam. She was the happiest I'd ever known her when she was with him. I was thrilled when she said she was pregnant. He was great with her and he asked her to marry him right away. Not out of necessity or anything either, I don't think. He loved her. Then she started to get these awful anxiety attacks. I thought it must just be the hormones. They can do that. I took her to see a doctor but of course she'd suddenly be absolutely fine. She told him I was over-reacting and she was dealing with it. They were very good actually, but what could they do if she didn't want help or seem to need it?

I convinced myself I was indeed over-reacting and your Grandad wouldn't hear it, which didn't help. He said I was being ridiculous and making her more anxious.'

'Must have been awful', I said, suddenly filled with empathy for her. 'Did my Dad see her like that? Is that why he left, do you think?'

'Do you know, love, I have no idea. I didn't want to mention it to him in case he really had no idea and it scared him off, and to be honest I was starting to think I was being silly because she seemed to pick up all of a sudden.' She took a deep breath. 'Well, they're clever you see. Good at hiding what's really going on in here', she said, tapping her head. 'I think Adam leaving was just the last straw. Pushed her over the edge and she was sitting pretty precariously as it was, I think.'

'Did you blame yourself?' I asked, and then immediately regretted saying something so insensitive. 'Not that it was your fault, Gran.'

'Well I did, I suppose. I thought I ought to have known. I should have ignored your Grandad and gone with my gut. Because really, I knew something was very wrong. I just didn't want to admit it to myself and I didn't want to fall out with her. Especially not with you on the way.'

I had been so cruel to her last night. I felt bad for thinking it was all about me. Did I really need to know this? Wouldn't I have been better off as I was? Maybe she did do the right thing after all.

'Do you still? Blame yourself I mean?'

'No, not anymore I don't. I had to have therapy. Me and your Grandad almost split up. Might have been better if we had, actually. We never really recovered after it. I was angry at him, you see. And he was angry at himself. He never forgave himself, really. How could I tell you? I had intended to talk to you when you were older but then you got older, and older didn't seem old enough, you know? Once you tell a lie it's very hard to un-tell it. You start believing your own version of events in the end until it's almost a shock when you remember it wasn't like that at all.'

'How did she…?'

'Pills, so many pills. There was no chance of saving her even if we'd got to her earlier. I count it a blessing that she did it that way. At least she was with me and your Grandad.'

'Did you really lose all of the photos in a fire? I asked.

'No. I'm afraid that was another lie. I just thought I might break down and tell you if we started going through all of the old photos. I didn't want to burden you in the end. You were quite an anxious child yourself and I was, well, I suppose scared is the word. I thought what you didn't know couldn't hurt you and all that. I am sorry, love. It was stupid of me to think you'd never find out and now you have, and it wasn't even me that told you. You had to hear it from someone else... oh dear, poor Sarah.'

'I know, I did feel bad. I'll apologise to her. And I'm sorry to you, too', I said, holding her hand. 'I was horrible to you.'

'I'm sure I deserved it. I'm glad it's out in the open now. I'm not happy that I didn't tell you myself but it's a weight off my shoulders to be honest. You've been very grown up about it.

'Eventually', I smiled.

'Look, do you mind if we let it all settle and then perhaps I'll get the old photos down from the loft sometime and you can have a laugh at my ridiculous hairstyles?', she said.

'That sounds like a plan.' I replied. Somehow talking about it openly, I felt a sense of relief myself. Even though it was awful and tragic and a ton of other bad stuff, it was the truth and, as they say, the truth will set you free. I'd heard that somewhere. I wasn't going to brush it under the carpet, I wasn't going to pretend it hadn't happened, I was going to try and understand why she had done it and hopefully I'd find some peace in that.

## Chapter Thirteen

'I can't believe you're leaving', I said as Josh put his arms around my waist for one of the last times. 'Why do you have to go? Can't you stay with your Dad?', I asked with tears building in my eyes.

'No, Mum says no way. Don't think he'd want me anyway', he said. 'We'll still keep in touch, though.'

'You say that like we'll just be friends or something. Are you ditching me?', I cried.

'It's California, not bloody Cornwall, Mads', he said as I stopped even trying to stop the tears from falling. 'Maybe you can come and see me sometime.'

'Yeah like that's gonna happen. How am I going to afford to do that? It's not as if my crappy wage is going to pay my air fare, is it?', I shouted.

'Well, if it's gonna be like this for the next couple of months we might as well end it right now.'

'Oh yeah, that's right. That's probably what you wanted anyway.' I cried some more. Josh couldn't handle tears. Happy ones or sad ones, they were all the same to him. At that moment, I wanted him to feel uncomfortable. How dare Mrs. Howells be so bloody selfish? Didn't she know he had GCSEs next year? Didn't she care about his education? She shouldn't have had kids if all she cared about was her career. What was so great about California anyway?

'Calm down, will you?', he said, looking like he wanted to run as fast as his legs would carry him. 'I wish I hadn't told you now.'

'Oh what, you wish you'd waited until you were at the airport instead, do you?' I was being unreasonable, I knew that. After all, it wasn't his fault if his Mum had a new job and I should have been pleased for him. It was just that he'd become my Sophie. I'd come to depend on him. He was always there for me and I didn't ever think he wouldn't be. I was placing all of my happiness on one person again.

August came, and went just as quickly. Josh and I spent all of the time we could together during the holidays. I decided that it was pointless carrying on like I had been. A week of it and I started to panic he might find someone else less annoying to hang out with for the rest of the summer.

When the day came and him leaving was an actual reality, I barely knew what to do with myself. 'You will call me, won't you?' I asked. Well sort of pleaded. 'Don't forget about me.'

'How is that likely?', he laughed. 'You won't let me, will you?'

'Too right I won't', I replied, planting the longest kiss ever on his gorgeous lips.

'I'll miss you', he said as he held me tight.

'You too.' There was so much more I wanted to say but I bit my tongue. Sometimes less is more and I didn't want to come across as needy. I didn't want him to go feeling relieved. I wanted him to be devastated. He wasn't, of course, but he was a bit sad.

'Oh love, cheer up', Gran said. 'I know you're missing Josh, but I have to live with you and it's been almost a week.'

'You don't understand', I cried.

'I do, of course I do. You're not the only one to have felt this way, you know. I remember first love and I wouldn't wish it on anyone', she smiled.

'Sorry', I said sheepishly. 'I just miss him so much, Gran.'

'I know you do but moping about like this isn't going to make you feel better, is it?'

'Spose not.'

'Get yourself out, love. I'm sure Penny would love you to go and see her. Don't neglect your friends, will you?'

'No, I won't, I promise. But she's with Noah now and they're all loved up and everything and I just can't take it at the moment.' I'd feel a pang of jealousy every time I saw them giving each other the look, you know, the one just between them. The one that me and Josh used to give each other.

Josh was literally all I could think about. I wondered what he was doing, who he was seeing, where he was going. He'd only been gone six days, but it felt like much longer. He'd messaged me on SnapChat, but he said he was too busy to call as they were still unpacking. He said he'd try and call this Sunday. Try and call? I sulked. To myself of course, to him I was all yeah, no problem, call me whenever.

Everything seemed such a chore. Getting up in the mornings, going to school, making conversation, even. I just wanted to curl up under my duvet and forget about him. Yes, that's it. I wanted someone to give me a pill so that I could close my eyes and when I woke up I'd have forgotten all about him. Gran was right. Love sucked. If we finished for good then I was never, ever going to go out with anyone else for as long as I lived because I never wanted to feel like this ever again.

'On another note', Gran said. 'I know this is the worst time given how you're feeling, but well, Arthur.' She trailed off like it was okay to stop at that point because I wouldn't want to know.

'Yeah?'

'He sent me this', she said, passing me two pieces of lined paper covered in scrawly writing.

'And he expects you read this?' I smiled. 'Is it nice?' I asked.

'I suppose it is, yes. I'm not sure what to do about it.'

I set about trying to make out actual words from his nonsense writing.

*Dear Louise,*

*I'm sure by now you have put me out of your mind and I wouldn't blame you for one minute. I've never been a person who is comfortable with my own emotions. I was married for twenty-eight years to a woman who couldn't bear the sight of me and I became hard. When I met you, it was like a bolt of lightning. You're kind, generous, smart and funny. All of the things Marjorie was not.*

*You made me so happy, Louise. I can't fully explain why I did what I did and I'm sure I have no right to ask for your forgiveness, but on the off-chance you are able to forgive me then I would love to give us another try. I will, of course, fully understand if you decide to leave things as they are. Please do not feel obliged to answer me. I know I have no right to your love, but I promise to love you for the rest of my days on this earth if you can find it in your heart to give me another chance.*

*Yours, Arthur*

'Oh my actual God, Gran', I screamed. 'This is amazing!'

'Is it, love? I'm not so sure. What's to say he won't freak out again?'

'You have to give him a chance', I said with tears in my eyes. I was happy for her, really happy, but sad for me. It was no good anyone telling me I was only fifteen and there were plenty of fish in the sea. I didn't want to even think about other fish.

'Do you love him?', I asked.

'Yes.' She replied.

'Well then, what's the issue here?'

'He might do it again. There's every chance isn't there?', she asked, like I would know. Probably with all my experience of love now.

'He might, I suppose. It depends if you're more scared than hopeful.' I had no idea where that nugget of adult-sized wisdom had come from, but I was going to write it down for future use.

'Oh my word, Miss Beaven, get you, all grown up and full of insight', she chuckled. Seeing her laugh made the Josh stuff seem less important, somehow. In that moment, I was only concerned about Gran. I wouldn't even have worried if they decided to get married. Bloody hell, I was mature wasn't I?!

***Hey babe, how are you. All unpacked now and missing you like crazy. Xx***

Just like that, there it was. He said almost exactly what I'd imagined him saying to me but thought he wouldn't. I wanted so much to start typing my reply but I stopped myself. No, he could wait.

## Chapter Fourteen

'You haven't texted him back?', Penny asked. 'Really, why the hell not? You've been dying to hear from him for days!'

'I know I have but I can't text him back right away, or he'll think he can pick me up and drop me whenever he likes, won't he?'

'Josh isn't like that.'

'Well you don't know him like that, so you can't say he isn't. He kept me waiting all week', I replied, annoyed at her for thinking she knew him better than I did. 'I will reply, just later.'

'Up to you, but I wouldn't do that if I were you', she said.

'Well you're not me, are you?', I replied bluntly.

'Whatever.'

Gran was still considering Arthur's request for forgiveness. I was irritated with her, because I knew she really wanted to but she was being all... Maddieish.

I knew I was being childish, not answering Josh, but it was like it was impossible for me to do the sensible thing. The part of me that wanted to reply was being trampled on by stupid me and there was nothing I could do to make her be more reasonable. I wondered if my stubborn streak came from Mum. I thought about her a lot. Once I got my head around the fact that she'd chosen to leave me, I decided to read about suicide online. I discovered that she didn't really choose to leave me, it wasn't a choice like that. She wouldn't have even thought about things rationally, probably. At first, I was mad with her, but now I just feel so bad for her. She had been feeling that way and she hadn't talked to anyone about it. She kept it all locked up inside so that it could torture her and make her feel like she had no option than to do what she did.

### You Okay? X

Why couldn't I just type back, *Good thanks*? It was like the time on the bus, with Sophie. I couldn't get my thumb to move. It had a mind of its own or something. I felt a bit sick in my stomach when I shoved my phone into my knickers drawer. Why was I being so stupid?

I wondered how Gran was doing. I took my mind off my boyfriend - my ex-boyfriend – and thought about Gran's love life instead.

'Have you decided yet?', I asked as I poked around the cupboard for a Penguin. I knew there was one left because I'd hidden it under the Kit-Kats earlier. 'Did you eat the last Penguin?

'Oh yes, sorry love, were you saving it?'

'Yeah.' In that moment, I wanted a Penguin more than anything else I could think of. 'Never mind. Doesn't matter.' It mattered so much it wasn't even funny.

'There are Kit-Kats', said Gran.

'Yeah, don't want one. I wanted a Penguin.'

'Oh well, have something else then.' She said.

If only all problems were that easily solved, I thought.


'So?'

'Well, I suppose I'd be silly not to at least give him a chance', she said, looking at me for approval.

'I agree', I replied, giving it.

'Really? You don't think I'm heading for a complete disaster, then?

'I don't know. I shouldn't think so, but you'll never know if you don't give it a go, will you?'

'So grown up now', she said putting her hand up to my face. 'Who'd have thought I'd be coming to you for advice on men, eh?', she chuckled.

'I know, right!'

'I'll call him later. I'll suggest we take things slowly and see what happens.'

'Sounds like a good plan.'

'Okay, now get and answer that poor boy, will you, young lady.'

Poor Josh. He was making all the effort, just like I'd wanted and now I was ignoring him. For what reason? To make a point. But I'd sort of forgotten what point I was even making anyway.

*Hi! Sorry, lost my phone. I hope you are settling in now. Miss u 2 x*

I wanted to go on and on about how much I missed him and how I loved him like crazy, but I didn't. I was too scared to say all of those things just in case he freaked. Miss you is okay, but love is something else. We'd never said that word. I'd wanted to loads of times but it just wouldn't come out and now I thought it was probably for the best because he probably didn't feel the same anyway. He answered right away this time.

***Thought you were off me! Xx***

*Never! X*

**How is everyone?**

*All okay. What is the new place like?*

**Here look...**

Oh my god, it was amazing. So much bigger than his old house. It was all modern and there was a pool. My heart sank in that moment. *Why would he come back?* Even if his Mum lost her job or something. What was the point in staying in touch? I'd just get all insecure imagine him with other prettier American girls with long blonde hair and big shiny teeth. I didn't want to feel like this. I felt horrible all the time and I had a constant knot in my stomach.

*Lovely. How long do you think it will be b4 you get back home for a visit?*

**Only just got here!! Don't know. You missing me already then? ;)**

*Haha, maybe. Shall we have a break for a bit?*

**FFS you getting all girl on me again?**

*Lol! No just thought you might want to and it's GCSEs x*

**Maybe leave it until the end of exams** ☹

*Might be best.* ☹ ☹ *xx*

**Don't get off with Dan though, will you?**

*Huh?*

**He fancies you. He told Penny and she told me.**

*She didn't tell me!!!!! I don't even fancy him anyway. He's not my type. ;)*

**Good!!!!**

*I'll miss u* ☹ *xxxxxxxxxx*

**You too. I'll stalk your Instagram!!! Xxxx**

And that was that. I couldn't decide whether I'd done the right thing or not. I'd partly done it hoping he'd tell me he loved me, but I sort of knew that wouldn't be the case. I felt a bit sick and like I'd been punched in the stomach. I wondered whether I should text him back and say I didn't mean it, but how would that look? I thought. I felt a bit mad with myself for saying it and trying to be the sensible one in the hope that he'd come to his senses and confess his undying love for me. *But he's a boy and they don't do that*, I said to myself, sighing out loud. I'd have to find things to do, lots of them and maybe I'd flirt with Dan just for fun. He was quite good looking, and I was secretly quite pleased that he fancied me. I'd kind of imagined it would always be me and Josh and I'd never even considered other boys an option in any case. I supposed it wouldn't do any harm to maybe go out with someone else for a bit, just while Josh was away. I mean, I was only fifteen after all.

## Chapter Fifteen

'So, did he text you, then?' Dan asked, yanking my phone out of my hand. 'Just because that blonde bit dumped him, he thinks he can come back to you. Well, he can fuck off.'

'It's not like that. His Dad has just died, for God's sake. Of course he's gonna come back.'

'Yeah, well anyway, you can't see him. No way Maddie.'

'What? I'm going to the funeral with Gran.'

'No, you're not.' He said, throwing my phone onto the pavement in anger. 'It's not you, it's him I don't trust', he said as I ducked down to get it just before he stamped his foot into it, cracking the glass.

'What am I supposed to do now?', I shrieked, as tears started to roll uncontrollably down my face. 'Arthur bought it for me. It cost him a ton of money. Oh God what am I going to say happened to it?' I was sobbing and making sounds that resembled words, but I wasn't really sure if they were.

'Shit, sorry Mads. It still works, look.' He said, thrusting it as me. 'It's just, you make me so bloody mad sometimes. You're so naïve. You don't know what boys are really like. He's after you, I'm telling you he is, don't see him, Mads. Please don't go to the funeral.' He started crying too, because that's what he always did when he did anything that made me cry. He had this way of turning everything back around to him and I ended up feeling like the bad one every time.

'Don't cry', I said as I put my arms around his waist. I hated the fact that I couldn't say the right thing, ever. I always managed to make a mess of things when it came to us.

Part of me wanted to tell him it was over because I was exhausted all the time and I was sure I'd failed my maths GCSE because we'd had a huge row that morning. I couldn't concentrate and then I realised I'd got two pages stuck together and I missed a whole section. The problem was, I needed Dan. When it was good, it was amazing. He said he loved me all the time. Like probably six or seven times a day and he always texted me just before I went to sleep. I was lucky to have him, really. Lots of girls fancied him, even Penny. She was a bit gutted when he asked me out. The weird thing was, I wasn't all that into him at the beginning. I just said yes for something to do and because Penny had been getting on my nerves at the time. She'd developed this slightly Australian accent because her cousin Tamsin from Adelaide was staying for a couple of weeks. It was so stupid, it was obvious she was just making it up because she thought it was cool, but it was annoying. 'I didn't realise', she said, when I commented on it. Tamsin had only been here for four days at the time.

'You don't pick up accents when everyone else around you is speaking in English accents and one is speaking Australian,', I told her. She got all pissy with me and said I was just jealous because I had nothing going on and I was probably still sulking about Josh. So, when Dan asked me out, I was all 'So there, now look'. Tamsin went back, and she was talking English again. I didn't see her much. I didn't have time because me and Dan were trying to spend as much time in the holidays together as we could before I went to sixth-form and he went to college.

'So, you won't see him then, you promise?', Dan asked as I surveyed my face in a car mirror and rubbed at the last little bit of mascara that had become smudged under my left eye with the sleeve of my jacket.

'Say you swear, Mads.'

'I did say, didn't I?', I snapped back, still furiously rubbing at my skin and making it bright red in the process. 'God, look at the state of me', I sighed. 'I'm fed up with crying all the time.'

'Stop upsetting me, then. You only get upset because you know you've hurt me, then you feel bad, so you cry.'

That wasn't it, but I couldn't be bothered to argue the point. I'd never win anyway. 'Yeah, I know.'

'Come here', he said, pulling me into him. 'You know I love you, don't you? I tell you often enough. He never loved you. You told me, he never said it to you, didn't you?', he said, reminding me how idiotic I was to ever think Josh loved me.

'I know he didn't. Anyway, we were young, and I've grown up a lot since then', I said, recoiling a little from his grip. I got confused as to why I'd feel like that sometimes when I knew I loved him. It was weird.

'I have to go home. I want to have a shower and take all this crap off my face', I said, running my hands over my pink skin. I'd done the best I could, but it was still a mess. I wanted to go back home, to the comfort of Gran and Arthur. I couldn't believe I'd been so concerned about him moving in. He was amazing, and not just because he'd bought me an iPhone. *Shit, my phone....*

***Hey, Maddie! Can't believe I'm back. Wish it was under other circumstances but I'm glad to be here. Looking forward to catching up soon. Maybe before the funeral next week??***

***Josh xx***

As I strained to make out the words through the cracked glass, my heart skipped a beat. It was as if he'd never been gone. I wondered how he was feeling. I mean, his Dad had been ill for months but still, I don't suppose he ever really expected him to die. Gran said he was recovering pretty slowly, but he was getting better after the heart attack.

I almost contacted Josh when I heard about it, but I was scared Dan would find out and I didn't want there to be a massive drama or anything. Anyway, Josh was still with Meredith, so I decided to leave it. I felt pretty bad, actually. It wasn't like we'd fallen out or anything.

He was really good about Dan and me. I didn't want him to know because I didn't see a reason to tell him. It wasn't as if we were in contact and I was worried he'd think I was only seeing Dan to provoke some sort of reaction. I wasn't. Actually, a reaction was the last thing I wanted. Dan thought it was best to be open about it though, so he posted a picture of us both and then texted him to say we were seeing each other and he hoped Josh was okay with it. Josh said he was and then a few weeks later his profile picture changed to the one of him and who I now know to be Meredith on some beach somewhere with a dog. I was surprised because Josh didn't really like dogs and especially not big ones like the one in the picture. They were laughing, and he looked happy. I did feel a little bit hurt, but then I told myself I had no right because I was seeing his best friend… ex-best friend… so what did I expect? I did find myself wondering how long they'd been together and studying her face closely to see if she was as pretty as me. Penny said she was very American and her teeth were probably veneers or implants or something.

Dan said we should get engaged but I said we were too young. We might drift apart now we weren't at school together and anyway, I wasn't sure I wanted to get married. He said that it didn't mean we had to get married, just that we were official and when boys saw my ring, they'd know not to approach me. I wasn't sure I didn't want to be approached by boys, to be honest. I didn't tell him that, though. Sometimes I'd see him looking at me if a good-looking boy walked past or got on the bus. I'd purposely look out of the window in case he thought I might fancy him. He was very possessive. I think it was because his Mum left when he was about ten or eleven. She went off with some bloke from Sainsbury's and Dan wouldn't see her when she tried to get back into contact. He'd never had contact with her since and I didn't think he even knew where she lived now.

*Really sorry about your Dad. Not sure I can make the funeral. Still got two exams left so revising like crazy. Hope you're okay.* ☺

I'd so wanted to send him a kiss, a hundred kisses if I was honest. I couldn't show any sign of affection though just in case he showed it to Dan, although I didn't really think he would.

**Can't you just meet me for coffee. I'm free tomorrow morning if you don't have an exam. Xx**

What harm could coffee do? Anyway, Dan needn't know. He had a biology exam in the morning and I didn't think it ended until eleven thirty at least.

*10 then. Starbucks? X*

Shit, I did the kiss without even thinking. God, I hoped he hadn't read anything into it.

**Can't wait to see you xxxxxxxxxxxxxxx**

# Chapter Sixteen

I'd turned my wardrobe inside out trying to find something that said sophisticated almost sixteen year old, but everything was old and boring and I hated it all. There was not one thing I wanted to wear.

Well, I couldn't very well turn up in my underwear, could I? I looked at myself and smiled. Who'd have thought it? My boobs had started to grow when I was fourteen and a bit. I didn't even notice them getting bigger, it was like one day they weren't there and then one day they were. I mean, they weren't huge or anything, but they were a good size for me. Just right, Gran said.

I called Dan early to wish him luck. I did think about telling him I was meeting Josh, because well, why shouldn't I? I didn't, though, because I didn't want to make him mess up biology or anything. I told myself it was for his own good and what he didn't know couldn't hurt him. Anyway, I should be able to have friends that were boys as well as girls. Although, to be honest, he didn't much like me having either.

I was lying awake thinking about us. I loved him, of course I did. I said it to him every day. Mostly because he got all pissy if I didn't and I didn't like his moods. I used to think it was so cute that he got all jealous and possessive and only wanted me to be with him but lately it had been getting on my nerves and actually, making me feel a bit stressed out.

Penny avoided me when we were together because she didn't think Dan liked her. I told her he did, but he didn't. He said she interfered and he thought she wanted to split us up. I don't think she did, though. Well, she might have wanted us to split but she didn't ever say so. Actually, I thought we were drifting apart. She was more friendly with Trudy these days. I didn't really care all that much. It wasn't as if I didn't like her anymore or anything like that, I just wasn't bothered if I saw her or not. I still saw quite a bit of Darcie because she was going out with Joel Tavener and he was one of Dan's friends, but usually it was in a group rather than just the two of us. I didn't mind that, but I was starting to miss girly Saturdays, trying on makeup and spraying perfume testers in Boots.

I still missed Sophie. After so much time, you'd have thought I'd be over it, but I wasn't. I missed our friendship right at that moment. I wanted to talk to her, tell her how I was scared about meeting up with Josh again and ask her advice. Should I finish with Dan? I didn't really need to ask anyone that question. I wasn't myself when I was with him. I was trying too hard to please him when really, he should have been making more of an effort to make me happy. I don't think he even cared if I was happy or not. Oh, maybe I was trying to make myself feel less guilty about seeing Josh by making Dan out to be worse than he was. I suppose he wasn't any different to other boys his age. I just wasn't ready for all this serious stuff. Gran said there was plenty of time for all that when I was older. She said I cried far too much and if that's how he made me feel then he didn't deserve me. I hoped it wasn't always going to be like this. Did adults feel like this all the time and just have to put up with it because that's how life is when you're old? I felt depressed all of a sudden.

'Oh my God!', he said as he stood up to give me a hug. 'You look amazing!'

'Oh thanks, so do you', I replied. 'It's been ages.'

'Too right it has.' He pushed some hair over my shoulder and I sort of froze for a moment. 'Sorry, old habits', he said smiling.

'So, how are things?' I suddenly realised how stupid a question it was. 'God sorry, silly question. Sorry about your Dad', I said.

'Thanks. Hadn't seen him for ages. He wasn't interested really. Not since Julie and the kids moved in. He was still my Dad though, I suppose. Just thought I might feel more... upset. Mum says it hasn't hit me yet, but I don't know about that. Maybe.'

'That could be. When Gran told me about Mum, I thought I was okay for a while. She kept going on about how mature I was and how I was handling it like a grown up and then all of a sudden it was like something inside of me snapped and all I could think about was how she must have been in so much pain and how no-one helped her and if they had then she'd still be here...'

'Bloody hell, Mads. You should have called me. We always could talk about stuff like that couldn't we?', he said, putting one hand on my leg and making me feel weird. 'You're okay now though, yeah?'

'Yeah, pretty much. Gran took me to see someone. I think she was scared I'd do the same thing, you know, kill myself or hurt myself or something. She didn't say, but I could tell. It wasn't like that, though. I just got these stupid palpitations and sometimes I would feel really sick and wouldn't want to go out for days at a time.'

'Shit. So, they helped you then?', he said.

'Yeah, it was cognitive behavioural therapy. Helps to get you to think rationally and order your thoughts, you know that sort of thing. I thought she was going to expect me to talk about my childhood and make out Gran was abusive or something, but she was nice. I still go once in a while, if I feel like a top up, you know?'

'You can always talk to me', he said, squeezing my thigh. God, could this get any more awkward?

'Thanks, but I've got Dan so it's fine.' That was a laugh, I couldn't talk to him about anything other than him.

'Can't imagine he's much use!', Josh laughed. 'No offence, sorry. I just don't remember him being that type.'

'Well he's sixteen now. He's changed.'

'Okay, sorry. None of my business. You happy then?', he asked.

'I'm okay.'

'Not the same thing.'

'Isn't it?', I replied. 'Are you seeing anyone since, well, since you and she split up?', I said, deflecting attention away.

'She's called Meredith in case you didn't know.' He smiled at me. 'Nah. Not bothered. Anyway, not sure where I'm gonna be, am I?"

'What do you mean?'

'Mum doesn't want to go back, well, she has to for a while, but she doesn't want to renew the contract. Doesn't like the constant heat, she says.' He raised his eyes to the ceiling. 'What the hell is that all about? She'd rather be here in the pissing rain than California in 25 degree heat all year round. Still I'm not bothered. I miss England.'

'Oh right. So, you might, what? Move back to the old place? I thought your Mum sold it.'

'No, she rented it while the couple who were going to buy it were sorting some mortgage issue out and then they couldn't get one in the end, so they just carried on renting it and now Mum says it was for a reason. Like the universe was saving her from making it permanent because she'd started to have doubts. Some shit like that. She's into all that stuff.' He laughed again, and I thought about my magic for a second.

It was great having him back. It was as if he'd never been away and the past year hadn't happened at all. I so wanted to throw my arms around him at that moment. Thinking about Dan, I wanted to scream out loud. *I didn't want to be alone, boyfriendless again, so I'd jumped in at the deep end and now I felt like I was stuck with him.* I was all mixed up inside. I thought I loved him but, then again, it wasn't like this. Not like it was with Josh.

'So, you're happy with Dan, then?', he asked. 'Didn't think he was your sort. Wasn't that what you said?', he smiled.

'People change.'

'Not that quickly. And not that much actually.'

'You were gone, and he was there.'

'Wow, he didn't need many qualifications then', he laughed, loudly and contagiously. I laughed really hard. Harder than I had in a long time. It wasn't even that funny, but somehow it seemed like the funniest thing ever.

'Bloody hell, calm down will you. You'll do yourself an injury if you're not careful.'

He put his hand inside of mine and I felt an electricity I hadn't felt for a long time. 'I still love you, Maddie.'

'I didn't know you ever did', I smiled.

'He's not my mate anymore, so I can say it. You can do better. It might not be me, but you deserve better.'

'He's okay.'

'So okay is enough for you then?'

'Now you're making me feel like an idiot. Don't do that', I said, pulling my hand away from his.

'Okay, sorry. I'm out of order. Can we forget I said that?'

'Which part?'

'The last part. Not the other part. Don't forget that bit.' He said pushing his bottom lip out like a toddler. He used to do that. It always made me smile.

## Chapter Seventeen

'Get off, you're hurting me', I said as I tried to pull away from his tight grip. It was no use.

'You lied to me. Why did you lie to me?', Dan yelled loudly in my left ear and he continued to hold my arm with force. I could feel it bruising. I bruised easily. He knew that.

'I didn't lie to you. I didn't know. It was very last minute', I lied. 'Please Dan, you're really hurting me. Do you want to hurt me?' I asked, looking right into his eyes.

'Course not', he said, releasing me. 'It's just so bugging, when you do things behind my back. You know how I feel about you seeing him.'

'Yeah I do. But he's my friend. Why shouldn't I see him if I want to?', I asked defensively. I knew it was stupid, impulsive. I was goading him really. I wanted a reason to finish it. Not that this wasn't enough.

'No, he's not. He was your boyfriend. You can't be friends after that. No-one can.'

'Don't be stupid.'

He lunged at me again and pressed his forehead into mine. 'Don't call me stupid, alright?'

I pulled myself away and pushed at him. 'I don't want this anymore', I yelled.

'Don't say that.'

'It's over, Dan. You're a bully. If you really loved me then you wouldn't treat me like this', I said triumphantly.

I couldn't believe what I was saying. That's what he was. I hadn't thought about it before. At first, I was glad of his jealousy. I liked it because I felt wanted, special. That feeling didn't last. Pretty soon I felt like I needed him because he made me feel like I was nothing on my own. Josh coming back had made me realise that this was messed up.

'Please Mads, please don't finish it. I love you. You know I love you', he replied, trying to pull my waist into his.

'No. I don't want it. You don't love me. How can you love someone and treat them like this? You act like I belong to you or something', I said. I was determined not to give in, not to feel sorry for him if he started to cry. I expect he thought this was the same as every other time. But it wasn't. Usually it was just a threat. I never really meant it. I just wanted him to stop being an asshole.

'Please Mads', he begged as he tried again to grip my waist. 'Don't do this.' The tears were coming. I knew the signs.

'Don't cry. It won't make a difference. I don't love you, Dan.'

'You won't do any better', he said, immediately changing into something else. 'And if you think you're going to get back with him, then you can think again. I won't have it.' With that, he pushed me hard into Mr. Plummer's wall. My spine bashed into the concrete and I winced.

*It was over. Thank God.*

'Fancy coming over?'

'Can't. It's Trudy's Birthday. We're out for drinks. Got some fake ID from my cousin and her mate', Penny giggled.

I didn't even know it was Trudy's birthday. Shit, I'd let everything go and for what? If things had been the way they were then, I'd be out pretending to be eighteen with them.

'Oh right. Not sure Trudy will pass for eighteen, even with ID', I laughed.

'I know, right?', she laughed, too. 'Still, I told her, we'll just have to do a runner if they start questioning us. You know what she's like under pressure.' She laughed again.

'God, yeah. She'll probably run as soon as they look at the ID!'

I'd forgotten what it was to have a laugh. I'd missed their company. I wanted to be going with them, but it was my own fault. I'd have to ease myself back in gently.

'Well, have a good time. Don't drink vodka. Remember what you were like when your mum and dad were supposed to be away that time, and then they came back because they'd had a huge row and you threw up on the new living room carpet?'

'Never again. Mum would kill me anyway. She threatened me with a baby sitter if I ever got drunk again. I think she actually meant ever too. We can't be back late anyway, so maybe just a couple of ciders.'

'Might be best', I giggled. 'Let me know how it goes.'

'Will do. You not seeing Dan tonight then?'

'Nah. Finished it actually.'

'No way! Never thought that would happen. I can say he's a complete twat now then?'

'Yep.'

'You can do better.'

'Someone else said that too.'

'Did they? Well you can, babe. He can't, though', she said. 'Speak soon, then.'

She hung up and I smiled. A proper, happy smile. I was going to get the old Maddie back once and for all, and I was absolutely never, ever, ever going to let a boy treat me like that again.

## Chapter Eighteen

No more GCSEs. School was out for the summer and all was well with the world. I was looking forward to the sixth form but, for now, I was looking forward to doing absolutely nothing for six weeks. I'd lie in until lunch time and go to bed in the early hours. I'd watch back-to-back episodes of all of the old 'Skins' seasons, even though I'd already seen them all. Gran said it was unsuitable, but all the best things are.

I pulled out the clothes from the bottom of my wardrobe. You know, all the crappy items you really should get rid of but never do because you can't be bothered to go to the charity shop and it seems like a sin to chuck them in the bin. As I pulled out an old pair of black jeans, out it came too.

Crashing onto the floor came the little pink box. I smiled to myself as I bent down to pick it up. I wondered if Mum had really only used it for earrings or had she made a wish or two. My smile dropped as I thought about how her life ended. She probably didn't have that sort of hope in her. *Maybe it is just a jewellery box*, I thought, stuffing it to the back of the wardrobe. For just a moment, I thought about writing something down and pushing it into the slot. *Don't be stupid, Maddie*, I said to myself, pushing the door shut. I started to fold my clothes up and put them into a black bin liner. I did rescue a little red dress I'd forgotten all about and a pair of grey jeans that were two years old but still fitted me.

'You seeing Josh again today, love?' Gran asked, as I came down with the red dress on. 'You look lovely. Haven't seen that dress in ages.'

'Thanks', I said, spinning around.' 'What do you think, Arthur?'

'Very nice, Maddie. You look very pretty', he said, looking over the top of his newspaper. That always made me laugh to myself for some reason.

'Thanks to you, too', I smiled, before heading into the kitchen. 'And to your question, Gran', I shouted, 'Yes, I am seeing Josh today'.

'Thought so. You be careful. Don't want that Dan getting all worked up again. He's a bit unstable that one. I always thought so.'

Dan had seen us out last weekend. He went crazy. He punched Josh right in the face, and he fell to the floor. More with shock, I think. He kicked me over as I bent to check on him. Gareth Browning and Jamie Marcombe had to pull him away. Josh wanted to retaliate but I begged him not to.

'Don't provoke him anymore, please Josh!', I pleaded. 'He's not worth it anyway', I said.

'No, he's not', he replied as I supported him back to his feet.

'I wish he'd just meet someone else', I said with exasperation. 'That would be easiest for everyone.'

'Can't see that happening anytime soon. He's so into you, it's crazy.'

'Thanks', I said sarcastically.

'You know what I mean!', he laughed. 'Anyway, it's not even as if we're going out is it?'

'It doesn't matter to him. He wouldn't believe me if I said we were just friends anyway.'

'Remind me why that's the case again?', he said.

'Because it's too soon and I didn't want to wind him up.'

'And how is that working out for you?', he said as a smile spread across his reddening face.

'Oh God, look at your face.' I said, ignoring his question. 'I'm so sorry.'

'Not your fault, is it? He's bloody lucky you stopped me from hitting him back even harder.'

'I don't want you fighting over me. It's not cool.'

'Thought girls loved that sort of thing', he laughed.

'Not this girl.'


'Meant to tell you', he said as we were walking home. 'Spoke to that Sophie girl yesterday.'

'Sophie?'

'Yeah you know, your ex-best friend, the one you binned off for Penny.'

'Oh my God, don't say that. I did no such thing. Well not exactly', I replied defensively. I did, of course. When you look at it, I ditched her.

'Why were you talking to her?' I suddenly had this sick feeling in my stomach that he was into her or something.

'She was waiting for her Mum in A&E when I went in with Mum. You know, when she cut her finger. She said hi and we got talking. She's really nice.'

'Yeah, she is', I said, pushing my arm through his. 'What did she say? Was she horrible about me?' I don't know why I asked. I knew she wouldn't have been.

'Not at all. She doesn't seem the type. She was telling me how they're moving to Dundee in September. Did you know that?'

'No, no, I didn't.'

My stomach flipped as the realisation that I'd probably never see her again hit me. I guess I'd always hoped that one day we might bump into each other in town or something, and we'd both say how we'd missed each other and that would be it. We'd be besties again, just like that. Now it was never going to happen.

'Did she say why?'

'Yeah, her Mum's new bloke works there. Not sure if she said that's where he was from, but yeah, that's why.'

I didn't even know Mrs. Guthrie had a boyfriend. These are things I would have known if we were still friends. Then again, if we were still friends, how awful would it be to lose her now? At least she was already gone, for me at least. Perhaps it was for the best. I could move on properly if she wasn't around. I wouldn't have to see her getting on with her life, hanging about with girls that weren't me. I did a good job of convincing myself it was all for the best.

I had wished for a Dan-free day today.

'Wow, you look amazing', Josh said as I walked towards him. 'Bloody hell Mads, you gotta stop doing this to me', he laughed.

'This is just some old thing I found at the bottom of my wardrobe, it's nothing special', I replied. I knew I looked good in it. Better now I'm almost sixteen. Next week, actually. *I don't feel any different.* I thought. I was sure that turning sixteen would be some sort of turning point, like something monumental would happen to me or something. Maybe I'd feel like a proper adult or I'd attain some marvellous insights all of a sudden.

'Yeah, right', he said, as he grabbed my hand in the same way he used to do. 'Come on, I said we'd meet Mum at one.'

We were having lunch with his Mum. I'd always liked Mrs. Howells. She treated me like a grown up and always asked my opinion about things. She was very pretty for an old person. She must be at least forty now, I should think. I couldn't imagine being forty. I could barely imagine being twenty. People probably expect you to be all mature and sensible by then.

'Where are we going?'

'Nando's.' Everyone from school went there. We'll see someone for sure, I thought. I prayed Dan wouldn't be there. In fact, I worried about it all the way there and even while we were sitting, waiting. I imagined him walking in and starting something. How embarrassing would that be? I thought. By the time we'd ordered dessert, I'd forgotten all about him.

'Great dress, Maddie', said Mrs. Howells. 'I've got one similar. Not so short, of course', she smiled. 'You have great legs, you're lucky. Mine aren't great. In fact, they are the worst part of me.'

'No, they're not!', I replied. Actually, I'd never set eyes on her legs, she always wore jeans.

'Very kind of you, but yes, they are. That's why I'm never out of these bloody things', she said, as she gestured at her legs. 'I'd love to get them out, but I wouldn't want to scare the neighbours', she laughed.


Eating with them reminded me of when we were together. Mrs. Howells liked to eat out at any opportunity. Josh said she couldn't cook to save her life and she didn't want to learn, either.

Just as I was throwing back the dregs of my lemonade, there he was. I mean, what the actual…

I didn't recognise the girl he was with. She was pretty with long brown hair curled perfectly and tied back loosely at the side. I can never get that look to go right. She definitely wasn't from St Stephen's. He looked right past us. He saw us but didn't acknowledge us in any way. So, he had another girlfriend? Some girl who didn't know any better, or didn't care what he was like.

'Well, maybe he'll leave you alone now, then', Josh said as we stood outside of Superdrug waiting for Mrs. Howells. 'Personally, I didn't find you that easy to forget about', he smiled.

'Well, I don't care, I hope he is over me. I can't even imagine what I was thinking of. I didn't even fancy him.'

'You are an idiot', he said, playfully pinching my arm. 'What about giving us another chance now he's out of the picture?'

'I'm playing hard to get. Can't you tell?'

'Yeah. You're pretty good at it.'

'I know. If you've got staying power, then maybe you'll get lucky someday', I said.

'Oh, I've got staying power', he replied, putting his arm around my shoulder. 'Bet I've got more of it than you. You'll give in to me sooner than you think.'

'You're that sure of yourself, are you?'

'Yep.'

'So, what's going on with you two then?' Mrs. Howells asked as we walked to the bus stop. We looked at each other and laughed. 'What? What did I say? What's so funny?'

## Chapter Nineteen

*What possessed me to do this, what was I thinking?* I'd been thinking about Mum a lot. Not just musing about our life together, if she hadn't done what she did. I mean, really thinking, deeply.

I was having recurring thoughts that I hadn't been enough for her, that she hadn't really loved me at all, that maybe it was my fault. I woke up one morning, after a particular anxious night and thought, I need to do something to help other people feeling like this, people who this has happened to, children, teenagers of parents that took their own lives.

'You don't need me.' Sarah said, as I begged her some more.

'Please, please, pleaseeeee...'

'I can't contribute anything lovely, can I?'

'Yes, you can. You were there, I wasn't. How can I tell people how they should be feeling when I didn't even know about it for almost fifteen years?'

'It's not about telling people how they should feel though, is it? Everybody's different. No one person will feel the same as another… probably. Or maybe varying degrees of the same, perhaps', she answered.

'You see, I wouldn't think stuff like that. I'm young and inexperienced.' I put out my bottom lip for the second time. 'I'm sort of regretting the whole bloody idea. Maybe I should just stop before I make a complete idiot of myself.'

'It's just local radio, Maddie. They'll be gentle with you. I'll be waiting outside. I won't go anywhere. Maybe they'll let me in the studio, you know, where they record. Would that help? I can ask if it would.'

'Yes, that really, really would help', I said with relief. Not much of it, I was still absolutely terrified. What if I started crying randomly and uncontrollably? I was feeling pretty emotional. What if I couldn't speak, like stage fright or something? That could most definitely happen. Oh god, I think that's what will happen.

'Look, you've come this far haven't you. The website looks fantastic, and you did that all by yourself, didn't you?'

'Yeah, but that was different. I'm good at stuff like that.'

'And the rest will come. You can't get better publicity than this, Maddie, and it's free', she said, kissing my cheek. 'Come on, pull yourself together. It's your birthday after all. Don't think about it until the morning. There's nothing you can do about it anyway. Worrying about it all day and night isn't going to change anything. It will, however, make you feel rubbish', she said, as she handed me a package, covered in gold paper, expertly finished off with a red bow in the corner.

'It looks too pretty to break', I said, picking at the tape. 'I bet I know what it is.'

'I bet you do, too', she smiled.

'I knew it!', I screamed, as I pulled the paper apart to reveal the gold dress I'd pointed out to her in H&M the week before.

'It's too expensive', I'd said, as she picked it up and studied it. 'I'll wait and see what money I get next week.' I had a feeling she'd go back for it because she'd commented that there was only one size eight left.

How long was long enough? I knew I wanted to get back with Josh, but I want to do it on my terms. Only I'd sort of lost any good reason to stretch it out any longer. I'd forgotten what my terms were, or if I even had any. Perhaps I was just waiting for him to beg. Did I really want that sort of boy though? Begging wasn't really Josh's thing, anyway. If I left it too long, he might find someone else. Girls like him. He's easy to like.

'Ooh, looks fabulous love', Gran said as I curtsied to her. 'That was very kind of Sarah, wasn't it?'

'Yeah, it was. She is very kind.'

'Yes, she is. I'm so sorry I didn't bring her into your life sooner', she said, with tears in her eyes.

'Don't worry, Gran. Don't be upset. I'm happy', I said, gripping her hands. 'Actually, I'm really happy.'

'Yes, you are, aren't you, love? I'm so very proud of you. I don't think I said.'

'I know you are. Anyway, you say it all the time', I laughed.

'I know. But I mean, about this. What you're doing I mean. I haven't spoken much about it, have I? I don't know why. I still find it hard, I suppose, even after all this time.'

'That's okay, Gran. She was your only daughter. Sorry if I didn't include you more. Maybe I should have. I hope you didn't feel left out or anything. It's just, well, Sarah sort of pushed me into it, really. Not that I didn't want to do it. She just got all enthusiastic when I said about it. I think she's bored now she's not working. It was a project for her', I said, apologetically.

'It's fine, love. I'm glad she's helping you with it. It's probably been good for her. I'm not sure what, if any help, she had at the time.'

'She saw someone. A counsellor, I mean', I said.

'Did she? Good, I'm glad. I should have known that', she said, letting out a sigh. 'I hope you didn't mind us giving you money this year, love. It's just that I don't have the slightest idea what to get you these days. This way you can get something you really want.'

'Money is fine. More than fine. Thanks.'

'I thought I'd feel different, but I don't. Did you?', I asked Josh as we wandered along the canal path. I didn't even care that I was overdressed.

'Not really. Do you want to feel different then?', he asked, nudging me slightly.

'Yeah, I suppose I do. I want to feel mature and adultish', I laughed.

'Really? Why would you want to feel like an oldie?'

'Not like old or anything, just a more grown up version of me or something.' I didn't really know what I was talking about. It seemed stupid now. Who cared how I felt? I didn't really.

'Eighteen. That's when you'll be a full-on adult. We've got a couple of years to be carefree and still get away with messing up once in a while.'

'Oh, that's a good way of looking at it.'

'I'm full of good ideas. Here's another one for you. What if we give it another go? From today, we are a couple again. Probably won't work out, but you never know', he laughed loudly, and I joined him.

'Oh, go on then.' I said as I stopped and pulled him into me. 'Gonna kiss me then, Howells?' I couldn't believe I'd waited so long to let him do that. It was so much better than it was with Dan. He was just a distraction until this. A crappy one as it turned out.

'Here you go', Josh said, handing me a neatly wrapped box shaped parcel covered in pink Happy Birthday Sixteen paper. 'Hope you like it.'

'It's not an engagement ring is it?', I laughed. 'Bloody hell, it's not, is it?'

'Course not.'

'Good. You got me worried there for a second.' I tore at the paper. Inside was a black velvet box. The sort of box a ring would be in. 'So, it's definitely not a ring?', I asked again.

'Look at it!'

'Sorry.'

I opened the hinged lid. Sitting neatly and beautiful pressed into the spongy centre was a shiny silver ring. 'It's nice.'

'Definitely not an engagement ring, though', he smiled. 'It's an eternity ring. See' He said, taking it out and thrusting it at me. 'Look, I got it engraved.'

### Josh and Maddie Forever

'Ah, that's so lovely.' I flushed a little as he put it on my finger. It was the perfect fit. 'How did you know? Or is it just a coincidence?'

'Your Gran gave me one of your plasticky things. I took that.'

'Plasticky things? I don't do plastic', I laughed.

'Well, you know what I mean. One from New Look probably.'

'I love it', I gushed as I kissed him hard on the lips. 'Thank god it's not an engagement ring though.'

'You don't want to marry me then?' He did the thing with his lip again.

'Don't want to marry anyone. Don't take it personally.'

'Well, I do take it personally', he said as he grabbed my hands. 'You'll change your mind one day.'

'Maybe.'

# Chapter Twenty

'Oh god, why did I ever agree to do this?' I berated myself as I sat with Sarah, waiting to be called in for my interview. Live interview, I must add. I can't even try again if I mess up. *I will mess up,* I concluded.

'Calm down, Maddie', Sarah said as she pressed her hand into my shaking leg and held it still. 'You'll be absolutely fine. Just keep telling yourself that. Say over and over in your head I'll be fine, I'm a confident girl. I do that all the time if I'm worried about making a fool of myself. I swap the girl for woman, of course', she chuckled.

'Does that stuff really work, then?' I was skeptical about affirmations. Weren't they just lies you told yourself to feel better?

'It does for me. Can't hurt, can it?'

'I'll just be lying to myself, though.'

'Fake it til you make it, that's what they say. Anyway, what harm can it do?'

*I am confident, I can do this, I am confident, I can do this, I am…*

'Right Maddie, you can come in now.' A man with thick rimmed glasses and a mass of blond hair smiled at me as he held the door open. I'd been talking to myself for almost ten minutes. I hadn't even realised. I felt better.

Geoff was nice. He made me feel comfortable and I stopped focusing on all the people listening to me. I felt like it was just us. Anyway, I could see Sarah through the glass and she kept sticking her thumbs up, so I assumed I was doing okay.

'I hadn't realised how much it had affected me', I continued, as Geoff nodded at me encouragingly. 'It was then that I decided I wanted to help other kids going through the same stuff. I mean, it wasn't so bad for me because I didn't even know my Mum, but it was still horrible to know she'd done that. Imagine how it is for kids who have grown up with their Mums and then had to deal with this', I said, as tears welled up in my eyes. I brushed them away quickly.

'Well I think it's an amazing thing to do, Maddie. Well done you. Teenagers get so much stick these days', he said.

I was wired. I wanted to yell at the top of my voice. I can do anything! I didn't know what I had been worried about. stick these days. It's good to see another side of them.' Geoff continued as he thanked me and put on the ads. 'Well done. You did great', he winked at me.

'Thanks!'

I mean, I could barely remember one actual thing I'd said, but I knew I was okay. Maybe I'd get into radio when I left school. Suddenly, thoughts of uni seemed a distant memory. Something I was never actually sure I wanted anyway. It was just something you did if you were clever. I used to be ashamed of being clever, I tried to cover it up and dumb myself down to fit in a bit, although I never really did. Not until I accepted myself, that is.

I felt a sudden urge to go home and watch old *Star Trek* episodes on Sky, even though I'd probably watched them all a couple of years ago, when my geek was in full swing and I had never considered it ever wouldn't be. It's not that I wasn't happy at that point. Actually, I really was. It was just that I'd started to remember the old me. And I was coming to the conclusion that she wasn't all that bad after all.

'You were awesome', Josh said, as he almost squeezed the life out of me. 'You sounded dead posh and everything.'

'I am dead posh', I laughed, forcing myself from his vice-like grip. 'Too posh to be dining in Burger King.'

'You snob', he joked. 'You know you love a good burger.'

'Yeah, you're right. I do. But some day, Mister, you'll be taking me to The Ivy.'

'Where's that?'

'Not here, that's for sure', I said, pushing him towards Derrick Gardner who worked there in the holidays. I was lucky to work where I did. No-one saw me. I was tucked away discretely in the back with no chance of embarrassment.

'Hi Derrick', I smiled.

'Hi.' He blushed bright red. 'What can I get you?'


'Oh love, you were fabulous', Gran gushed as Arthur nodded in agreement.

'Yes, you were', he said. 'Like a proper celebrity now', he chuckled. 'Cup of tea?'

'Yeah, great.' I felt like I should be drinking champagne. I was still on a high. I needed to come down to earth before I had a horrible accident due to all my pride overwhelming me. God might think, that's enough now, Madilyn. I didn't want to get all big headed and up myself. It was only local radio after all, not Big Brother.

'I thought Sarah might have stayed on a bit', Gran said.

'She had to get back. She has an interview in the morning.' All of this website stuff had made her want to get back to work, she'd said. She had decided that she wasn't designed to be a stay-at-home Mum. She said it was harder than working, at her age. Her Mum had agreed to look after baby Evie three days a week. I don't think Darren was very happy about it. He didn't get on with her Mum.

Marriage seemed complicated. I didn't think I'd bother with it, myself. I wasn't sure how Darren felt about Sarah spending time with me. I felt like he didn't like me all that much. Sarah said he was just grumpy anyway. Like, all the time, so not to take it personally. I thought it was mean of him. Not about how he was with me, but that he was grumpy all the time. He should have been looking after her and treating her well. It was him who had wanted her to have a baby anyway. She told me she'd have been happy to never have had one. *I don't think I'll have one.* I decided. It seemed like you had to give up everything nice and look after them and your husband. Josh was right. Why be in a hurry to grow up?

# Chapter Twenty-One

'I can't believe we're saying goodbye again', I sighed as I looked him in the eyes for the last time once again. The funeral had been yesterday. It was even more depressing because he was going away again. He didn't cry but lots of people did. His Dad's brother read a poem and so did his ten-year-old step sister, Lilly. Watching her up there trying to be all grown up and struggling to stop her bottom lip from trembling, I wanted to run up to her and throw my arms around her. *Why isn't anyone rescuing her?* I asked myself as she started to fight back tears. I can't imagine how she got through it, but she managed it. I looked over at Josh, expecting him to be holding back tears of his own but he wasn't.

'Don't go finding yourself another boyfriend this time, will you?', he smiled.

'Not a chance. Even though it's only two months, it feels like a lifetime. What if your Mum decides to stay after all?' That could very possibly happen. Mrs. Howells was always changing her mind about stuff. Gran called her flighty.

'I'm coming home whatever happens. I have to get my GCSEs next year. I'm gonna be behind everyone else', he said, putting both hands behind his head. 'I'll move in with Nan. She said it's okay. It's not the best solution ever though. You know what she's like. She'll be setting me curfews and getting me to put shelves up and cut the grass and things.'

'Small price, Howells', I said as I pulled him into me. 'I'm worth it.'

'I know you are. Anyway, I can't see Mum not coming back, unless she hooks up with some guy.'

'Well, make sure she doesn't.'

'I'll try.'


It felt different this time. Even if he didn't come back, I knew I'd be okay. I'm not quite sure how I knew this, I just did.

Dan hadn't bothered us since the cinema incident. I guess he was with that girl, now. It's funny how you can just stop loving someone. Maybe I hadn't loved him after all, though. I think I was trying to love him, rather than letting it happen naturally. It wasn't like that with Josh.

I'd hate to be a year behind with everything. He's almost wasted the past year. Not that it's his fault, that was down to his Mum. I liked her a lot, I really did, but she was one of those people who just did what they wanted, no matter how it affected other people. When she'd had enough, she wanted to come back, and stuff her son's education, well that's what Penny's Mum said, anyway. Not that I wasn't glad she decided to come home. I wondered if I'd still be with Dan if he hadn't come back. I wanted to think that I would have come to my senses anyway, but I'm not sure that I would have, to be honest.

I couldn't believe it was that time already. Results day had seemed like forever away and now it was here.

'What do you think you got?', Penny asked excitedly. 'I reckon I got an ungraded in maths. I'll probably have to take it again next year. Stupid, I'll only fail again. Mum says if you're no good at maths then you'll always be no good at maths. I'm a words person. Not a numbers person.'

'Dunno. I stuffed up with my paper. I got two pages stuck together so I missed a whole bloody section. I think I did okay in English though, and history. Not sure about the others.'

I knew I'd done okay. I didn't want to make an idiot of myself just in case. And besides that, I didn't want to boast. Penny isn't an academic person, that's what her Mum says. 'You're more of a practical girl' she said when Penny was stressing about what she was going to do in September. It had already been made clear to us that we had to get B's and above to stay on. I would have been surprised if Penny had managed a B in anything.

'I might just go travelling, anyway', Penny said. 'I've got that money Nan left me.'

'Really? Would your Mum let you do that then?', I asked.

'It's not up to her, is it?'

'But you're only sixteen.' She didn't mean it, I thought. She was just saying it because she thought she wasn't going to do very well.

The queue for our brown envelope was a long one. I'd wanted to get here earlier to avoid the masses. I wanted to come on my own too, but Penny wouldn't hear of it.

Darcie couldn't get here until later because she'd just got back from Spain, so I couldn't very well not come with her. I was worried I'd do really well and she wouldn't. I didn't want her to feel bad.

I didn't recognize any of the women sat behind the desks. They were handing us our future in an envelope. I felt a bit sick all of a sudden. What if I hadn't done as well as I thought I had? I had no idea what I wanted to do. I was just going to sixth form to give myself some thinking time. I'd chosen English, History and Biology at A level. God, three A levels, what was I thinking?

'Name and class please?' The lady with the red hair, cut into a sharp bob looked up at me and smiled.

'Maddie Beaven, SG11'

She started searching through the green box that was stacked with crisp, brown envelopes. I wondered how many people would be disappointed. 'Here you go Maddie, good luck.'

I waited while she found Penny's envelope.

'Here we go, then', she said, linking my arm as we wandered along to the atrium where there were small groups of people huddled about. A couple of girls were crying. Miss Ludlow had her arm around some girl I recognised from the middle set. I heard a loud excited cry from the group at the far end and laughter from a large group of boys taking over the middle section.

'You go first', said Penny. 'Or shall we do it at the same time?'

'Same time.' My heart was beating right out of my chest and the palms of my hands were wet with sweat.

I tore at the envelope and stared at the little slip of paper. Two years of revision and it all came down to this. A scrap of white paper telling us if we were really as clever as we thought we were.

'Oh god, I can't look. Can you read mine for me?', Penny asked, thrusting her little slip of paper at me.

'I haven't even looked at mine yet. Anyway, I don't know if I want to read yours for you.'

'What, because you think I've done crap?'

'No, course not. It's just, well I don't know what you're expecting, do I?

'It doesn't matter. I don't even know what I'm expecting anyway. Go on!', she continued.

'Okay', I relented. 'You got a four in English, that's good. Oh, a one in maths, sorry.

'That's okay. I don't care about maths. I didn't even understand one single question, so I don't even know how I got that', she laughed. 'What about business?'

'Um', I scoured the list to the bottom. 'Oh, there it is, you got a D. Is that what you were expecting?' I knew she needed a C for college. She'd provisionally signed up for the business course.

'Shit, did I?' She looked gutted. 'Any other good ones?'

I was desperate to give her something. 'Here, here's a good one. You got a C in games, that's good.'

'Games, great. Where's that gonna get me?'

'It's better than nothing. Everything else is D and you got an E in religious studies.'

'That's me totally stuffed, then', she said. 'God knows what I'm going to do now.'

'Didn't you say there's another level?'

'Yeah, a lower level, trust me to end up there. Oh well, I suppose there's not much I can do about it now. I should have revised more. What about you?'

I scanned through the list, picking out just a couple to tell her about. 'Got a 4 in maths. That's pretty shit.'

'No, it's not. You managed that even with missing a whole sheet. I wish I was naturally clever like you.'

'I'm not', I said defensively. I had revised every night for the last six months of school. I'd worked hard. I was irritated that she thought I hadn't had to try. 'You could have done better if you'd revised', I said, and instantly regretted it.

'Yeah, well tell me something I don't know', she snapped back at me.

'Oh my God, sorry I said that. I didn't mean it.'

'Yes, you did. Anyway, you're right. I'm lazy, that's what Dad says. I deny it, but I am. I just can't be arsed with it all.'

I shouldn't have, but I started to laugh. It was quite inappropriate really. At first, she just looked at me. After a couple of seconds, she burst into fits of laughter.

'Do you know what? I don't really give a shit', she said. 'Is that really bad?'

'Yeah', I laughed some more. 'Anyway, you'll be fine. You always are.' She was one of those people who always landed on their feet. She was confident. When you're confident, you can probably do anything.

'Come on then, what else did you get, missis brain box?'

'I got an A in English language and English Lit, a B in biology, B in history, A in IT, B in business and a C in chemistry.'

'Bloody hell, you clever cow!' She smiled. 'Oh well, at least I have a clever friend. When you're rich and famous I expect you to remember your idiot friend', she laughed.

'You're not an idiot. You are smart, just in other ways. Some people aren't good at exams.'

'I know you're just trying to make me feel better. Oh well, at least Mum and Dad aren't expecting me to do any better. I hope they still take me out for dinner.'

'Course they will.'

'How did you do?' I heard a voice to the left of me, just as we were about to leave. 'Bet you did really well.'

It was her, Sophie. For a moment or two, I was speechless. I couldn't find one single word to say.

'Are you okay?', she asked, resting a hand on my arm.

'Yes, sorry. Um, yeah okay actually. How about you?'

'Not bad. I thought I might have done better in English Lit though. I might appeal it, Mrs. Havers says if I'm just a point or two from a five then I can. Not that it matters too much though. It's enough for college.'

'In Dundee?'

'Yes, that's right. What about you? Will you do A levels too?'

'That's the plan. Don't know about uni yet, though. Not sure what I want to do.'

'Me neither', she smiled. 'Oh well, I'm sure you'll do well whatever', she said. 'Bye then, Maddie.'

'Bye.'

I wanted to throw my arms around her and say I was sorry for treating her so badly.

'Good luck', I said instead.

'Thanks', she smiled, as she turned away from me for the very last time.

## Chapter Twenty-Two

'Your Mum would be so proud of you, Maddie', Sarah said when she called to tell me she was getting divorced. 'I wish I was as confident at your age, now even', she laughed.

'Thanks. But back to you. What about Evie?'

'Oh, she'll be fine. I won't stop him seeing her. He's done nothing wrong, not really. Apart from being a grumpy git, that is.'

She laughed loudly, and I winced as my eardrum vibrated.

'Still, I knew what he was when I married him, so it's my fault really. Don't marry for anything less than crazy mad love, will you Maddie?'

'You didn't, then?'

'Hell no. I married because my sister was getting married and all the attention was on her. I wanted some of it, I was jealous of her. How pathetic it seems now. I'd thought, oh well he's nice enough and he loves me. I'm not all that pretty and I might not find anyone better. Believe me, that is no good reason to walk down the aisle.'

'Hell no!'

'Anyway, don't do it for a few years yet will you. And don't get pregnant either.' She said, her voice suddenly becoming serious. 'You be careful, my girl. Don't give it up until you're ready and always use protection.'

'Oh God, please!', I shrieked. 'Not what I want to be talking about with you!' I giggled with embarrassment.

'Well, it needs saying. Can't see Louise mentioning it any time soon, can you?'

'No, thank god.'

'I feel responsible for you. I want to be responsible for you', she said. I felt tears prick my eyes as I let out a little cough to bring myself back to my senses.

'You don't have to be, though.'

'No, I know that. Like I said, I want to be. You're an absolute blessing, Maddie. I blame myself for not pushing Louise really. I ought to have gotten to know you sooner. I can't just put the blame on your Gran.'

'No-one is to blame. It's just what happened', I said.

'You're right. You're so grown-up now, aren't you?'

'Sometimes maybe.'

'Sometimes is good. Who wants to be grown-up all the time? Don't change, will you?'

'I'll try not to.' The funny thing was, I'd always wanted to change, to be someone else. Now I didn't. I was pretty happy being me. I'd gone back to watching all the geeky science stuff on YouTube and I'd started to write. I always used to think that I could never be successful like that. Not in a putting myself out-there sort of way. Since the radio thing, I'd come to almost love shoving myself into the limelight at any given opportunity. I don't think I was showing off or anything. I just wasn't afraid anymore.


Josh was due back in two weeks. I couldn't wait to see him. I'd gone past pretending I didn't care and trying to be all aloof. I didn't really have it in me, if I was honest. I always found it really hard not to be my full-on self. Like Gran said, if anyone doesn't want you for the whole person that you are, then they are not for you. She was full of little bits of wisdom like that. It used to annoy me, but now it made me smile.

Penny decided not to go to college after all. She couldn't face the consolation class, so she took a job in TopShop. She'd already started. I was actually pretty chuffed because she let me use her discount. She still wanted to travel but her Mum said she couldn't until she was eighteen. Working with clothes really suited her and she said that Sienna Miller had come in the previous week. I didn't think it was really her, but Penny was convinced so I didn't want to say it probably wasn't her.

I had no idea what I wanted to do, but I thought I might like to be a journalist. I wasn't sure when I had decided that, but it was there in my head anyways. Not the type who scraped the barrel for news. A serious one, reporting on proper news and maybe doing some of my own writing on the side. Something like that anyway.

Sarah got herself a job in a dental surgery. She was working on reception. She said Darren was giving her a hard time, though. He didn't even turn up to take Evie out last week like he had promised he would. I told her that he doesn't deserve to be in her life if he's going to carry on like that, but Sarah said he was her Dad and she was going to keep trying with him.

*Why do men have to be so difficult?* I thought. I hoped things never get like that with me and Josh. He wasn't like that, though.

Then again, maybe Darren hadn't been either. Perhaps you just became unreasonable when you got old.

I couldn't believe how much I missed Sophie. It was so stupid because I hadn't been getting around with her for almost two years. It was just that now she wasn't here, it felt like she had died or something. I'd lost all hope. Before, I had had this little bit of hope. She was still around and maybe something would happen, and we'd get back together again. Now there was no chance of that. It was all my fault. The whole thing, right from the start, it was all me. If only I'd apologised to her that day on the bus, if only I'd told her I was sorry on results day... if only...

I didn't think it was possible to un-stubbornise yourself. I found myself wondering if I got that from my Dad. Until now, I hadn't even considered trying to get in touch with him. But, in the last few days, it was all I'd thought about. Was he out there knowing about my existence and not even caring to find out if I was alright? Maybe he thought I'd been adopted or aborted or something. How could he not have tried to find out what happened to me as soon as he discovered what Mum had done? I'd been trying hard not to let it bother me, but it was getting the better of me. I'd switched all of my attention to him. I knew I'd have to do something about it or I'd drive myself crazy.

'I have no idea where he is, love', Gran had said when I'd broached the subject of looking for him with her a few days earlier. 'Sarah said he never came back home. She thinks he's still in Australia. It's not even as if his parents lived in Cardiff. Actually, I don't know where they lived. He'd moved to go to college and just stayed, I think.'

'Oh, I don't even know if I want to meet him, really. Maybe it's just a phase. I'll get over it, I expect.'

'Maybe. Look, why don't you let it sit for a while? See how you feel after Christmas perhaps', she said, handing me a hot chocolate covered in fluffy cream. 'Does that sound like a good idea?'

'Yeah, guess so.' She was probably right. I had this habit of over-thinking stuff and maybe I only wanted to see him to make him feel bad about Mum. I probably wanted to see him squirm. 'I'll try and forget about it for now, then', I said. For all of two seconds, I contemplated my little pink box again. *Stupid Maddie*, I said out loud. Magic is for kids.

## Chapter Twenty-Three

'Do you ever wonder if you're wasting your time because this isn't right for you?', I asked Taylor as we wandered into town on our lunch break. She'd become my new best friend, I suppose. I still saw Penny and Darcie a bit but not too much now. What with Penny working full time and Darcie at college, we all had other friendship groups. 'I mean, I'll be seventeen soon, and I have no idea where I'm going.'

'Nah, I don't worry about that stuff. Why do you need to know where you're going?'

'I don't know. I've always had some sort of a plan. Now I feel all mixed up and like I'm doing A levels just because that's what everyone expects me to do.'

'Well just do them and see then', she said. Taylor was a practical sort. She said it as it was, and she was probably right. What did it matter? I was still young. 'Anyway, what else are you gonna do?'

'Well that's just it. I don't know. It just feels like this isn't the right path for me, you know?' I couldn't explain it any other way.

Something just felt off. It was like there was something else for me. 'Don't you ever just get a feeling about things like that?'

'Not really. I just go with the flow and see what happens. You think too much, that's your problem.' She was right. I had a habit of over-thinking things.

'Spose.'

I had the website and I loved running that. Sarah helped me with the administration and checked for dodgy forum comments and that sort of thing. I mostly just kept it up to date. There were a few times that I felt compelled to comment on things, like if I thought I could really help, but mostly it was about letting people talk to each other. I'd put up links to other blog posts if I thought they might be helpful. I was proud of it. I was actually okay saying that too. 'I thought about doing something online. Maybe starting something else.'

'What, like the suicide site?'

'Oh my God, don't call it that!', I shrieked. As well as being practical, Taylor was also very inappropriate. She'd say things that other people would be careful not to say. She'd say them without considering them. She didn't have that part of the brain, the bit that filters stuff. 'No, I don't mean like that, I mean something businessish. To make money.'

'You want to be an entrepreneur or something?'

'Well, why not?' I didn't think that was what I wanted. I was probably too young to be one anyway.

'Do it, then', she said. 'Think of it this way, it doesn't matter if you mess up because you're still young and you get another chance', she giggled. 'Mrs. Branson.' She laughed.

'Very funny.' Maybe I was thinking too big, and anyway what would I do? I didn't really have any clue at all. If a feeling was anything to go by, then that's what it was.


Gran and Arthur had decided to make it official. She'd always said there was no point. I don't know when she changed her mind, but now it was all about the perfect outfit and wedding venues. Actually, it was quite exciting. I was enjoying helping her find something to wear. 'You need something that says sophisticated but still fun', I said as we browsed Marks and Spencer. 'Why don't you look online?'

'No, thank you. I like to try things on. How can I possibly buy something from a picture?'

'You can send it back if it doesn't look right. We can order lots of things and send back the rubbish stuff.'

'Oh, now that's not very ethical, love', she said, frowning at me.

'There's nothing wrong with it. That's what people do, they expect you to', I said.

'I don't know about that, love.'

'Well, just if we can't find anything suitable then.'

'Maybe.'

What was it about old people and the internet? It was like they thought it was out to get them or something. Gran said it was because it wasn't around when they were growing up. 'You hear terrible stories about people losing all their money. Terry Manners from the Post Office lost over a thousand pounds, and he knows about these things', she'd said when I had tried to get her to do her banking online.

'He probably did something stupid then. Opened a dodgy link or gave out his password.'

'I don't think so.'

'It only happens if you do something like that. If you're sensible, it's pretty secure.'

'Well, I'd rather not risk it, love.' I didn't imagine Gran had ever risked anything. I loved her to bits, but I didn't want to end up like her. I know how horrible that sounds, but I wanted more. I wanted to travel, to meet exciting people, to do things other people didn't do. Maybe I had something to prove to myself. Maybe I was scared of dying without accomplishing things. I'd become more concerned about time since I found out about Mum. Not taking my own life, I was over that concern now. More like the thought that we don't know what time we have left and what if it runs out sooner than I thought, and I'm left with regret?

'I'm not sure I can call Arthur Grandad. He won't expect me to, will he?', I asked her.

'I shouldn't think so love. He hasn't mentioned it.'

'Good. It's not me being funny or anything. I'd just feel a bit weird about it, that's all.'

'I'll have a word with him, don't worry about it.' I thought back to the time when I'd hated the idea of someone else in this house. Particularly a man. I didn't want things to change back then. I didn't care how Gran felt, it was all about me.

Now the idea of change excited me. The thought of things staying as they were was what scared me.

## Chapter Twenty-Four

I don't know why I hadn't really liked Christmas before now. Perhaps I felt differently about it this year because I was with Josh and the wedding was on the 12th January, so I had something extra to look forward to. I used to dread the lead up to it. Something about the fact that everyone seemed to pin the whole of their existence on those two holiday weeks. I always felt disappointed in it and then depressed when January came.

I found myself actually looking forward to it this time around. The crowds of people coming to see the Christmas market, the overcrowded shops and people banging into me with heavy carrier bags, none of that bothered me. I threw myself into it, behaving just like all of the other loons.

I found myself wondering what Sophie was up to. I'd thought about sending a card. I knew I could probably get her address from someone, but I was too scared. What if she didn't send one back? I'd sit sometimes, just daydreaming about us back in the day. I'd wonder how different my life would have been if we were still best friends. Then I'd get cross with myself because I really should let it go. *What was the point in wishful thinking?* My pink box had been sitting at the bottom of my wardrobe since I'd cleared it out. It was just a stupid bit of painted wood for earrings and necklaces. Admittedly, I hadn't put the wish inside of it, but it wouldn't have made any difference if I had. It seemed the more you wanted something, the further away it got, and Dundee couldn't be much further away.

I was thinking about Gran's suggestion. Putting Dad away until after Christmas. I'd been thinking about him on and off for weeks when Taylor suggested something so obvious, I couldn't think why I hadn't thought of it. 'Why don't you look him up on Facebook?', she said. 'All the oldies are on it these days', she laughed. 'Worth a try yeah?'

'Yeah, course I could. Didn't think of that!' I laughed loudly. 'Thank God for social media.'

'Let's do it now!' She squealed with excitement.

It was then that I was filled with a sudden fear. He'd already rejected me once. Was I prepared for him to do it again? 'He's probably not even on there.' I said, second thoughts overwhelming me.

'Well, we can at least try.' She said. 'What's his name?'

'Oh shit, I only know his first name'. I lied. I'll ask Gran.' At least I'd have some breathing time. I might consider it, but it wasn't something I wanted to do on an impulse, and definitely not here, with Taylor. It was too important.

Sitting there at my desk, writing out a card to Sarah, I thought about him again. Could I bear it if he didn't want to see me, or worse still, ignored me? What would I even say Hello, you don't know me but I'm your daughter. He might just think I was mad or something.

What if he had other children? What if I had brothers or sisters? I found myself feeling both thrill and terror at this prospect.

The niggling feeling just wouldn't leave me. I sat there for at least half an hour, just staring at my computer screen. Maybe I would just look him up, not message him or anything but just take a look. I tapped at my keyboard *Adam Matthews*. My heart was beating ten times faster than usual and I felt sick to my stomach. *Shit, what am I doing?* I said out loud as I clicked back to my own profile.

There he was, my Dad. I took a few deep breaths and then I went back and searched again. I knew it was him right away, even before I saw where he lived. He looked like me. I mean, really looked like me. Or I suppose I looked like him. It wasn't a similarity I had to look hard for. It was obvious. I had his nose, I smiled like him. He looked nice. He had a kind face and his eyes lit up when he smiled. They were sort of sparkly, I thought.

He was married, but I couldn't see any sign of children. His profile was open, so I could see all of his photos if I'd wanted to. It felt wrong somehow, sort of like I was spying on him or something. I'd made it a rule never to look at anyone's photos if I wasn't friends with them, so he shouldn't be any different. At least I knew he never came back. He probably met his wife and stayed. So, he didn't even try and come back to see me. My head was all mixed up. He looked so nice, yet how could he be?

I sat there for ages, just staring at his face. There was someone out there other than Gran who had my nose. He was my flesh and blood and yet he didn't want to see me. My Mum took her own life and my Dad got about as far away as he possibly could. If I was a more insecure person I might find that impossible to cope with. It wasn't impossible, but it wasn't easy either. I wanted to hate him, he deserved to be hated. But I didn't hate him. I had this weird feeling inside of me, like he was actually a good person. I had nothing to base that on, but somehow I knew it to be true.

I wasn't ready for him. Not yet. I knew where to find him, so that was something. I wrote down his wife's name and some of his friends, just in case he came off Facebook. He lived in Sydney and he was a marketing executive for a company called Blachford And Sweeny. I wrote it all down. I didn't look the company up, but I had everything I needed when or if I wanted to contact him.

'So, do you think you will, then?', Josh asked when I told him my findings.

'Don't know. Maybe.'

'What's stopping you?'

'Something. Not sure what. It just doesn't feel like the right time, you know?'

'I guess so. Oh well, at least you know something about him now.'

'Yeah. I just want to feel good about him. At the moment, I feel unsure. I mean, I feel like he's a good guy, but I might be wrong.'

'Your feelings have never let you down so far, have they?', he said. 'It freaks me out how you're always right about things', he laughed. 'It's like witchcraft.'

'Yeah, so think on!' I laughed, too.

I'd come to realise that, whenever I went with my gut feeling, premonition I suppose, I never went far wrong. Maybe there was a reason, and this wasn't the right time. Anyway, I had to work other stuff out just now. I wanted to know what I wanted. In career terms, I mean. I thought Taylor was probably right. I might just as well get some A levels under my belt. There wasn't much point in leaving school with nothing.

'Something to fall back on, love', Gran said, when I told her how I was feeling. 'You've only got just over a year to go now. No point jacking it in, is there?'

She was right, really. I was just longing to get on with something else. Only I didn't know what that something else was. I threw it out there: *Please help me discover what I should be doing*, I said out loud. I had no idea who I was making demands of, it just felt good. I felt a little bit of a release too. It was like it was in someone else's hands now. That was so stupid, I knew that. I was going with the relief though. I felt better.

## Chapter Twenty-Five

*I pull myself upright and shove two pillows behind me. I unfold all of the little slips of white paper. Reading them all to myself, I take a sharp breath. Wow, all but one of my wishes had come true. I have everything I've ever wished for. It was all here, in my own writing.*

*I look wistfully at the unfulfilled wish. Sophie... I wonder how she is and what she was doing. She'll be twenty-one now. She is a few months older than me. I wonder how she celebrated. I hope she is happy. That is my biggest wish right now. I hope Sophie is happy.*

*Was it really possible to wish a life into existence? It seems illogical to me, but that was exactly what had happened.*

*If I hadn't shouted out loud that day, if I hadn't asked some other force to help me, then what might I be doing right now? Would I be making money from my writing or would I still be at university wondering what on earth I was actually going to do with my life still?*

I remember it well. That day, just a few days after I'd shouted at the universe. I was sitting in English, staring out of the window while everyone else got on with their essay on the pros and cons of social media, when it hit me. I wanted to write for children. To make kids see that they were okay just the way they were. To teach them through stories that it was okay to be different. I was overwhelmed with excitement... no, momentum. In that moment, I knew that this was what I was going to do. I had no idea where to start or how I was going to get anyone to notice me, but I knew it was what I was destined to do. I knew I could write, and that was a good start. I'd finish my A levels, just in case, and in the meantime, in my spare time, I'd write. I'd do it for fun and see where it went.

It was around that time that he contacted me. It was almost as if my excitement brought him to me, or at least that's how it feels now, thinking about that time again.

'Can you come downstairs a minute, love?', Gran called to me one Saturday afternoon.

Just a minute', I called back as I finished the first chapter of my book. Typing the very last word of the introduction was an accomplishment I wanted to sit with for a few minutes. Looking at that word, I took a deep breath. I wondered if this was the start of things for me. Was this what I'd still be doing ten years from now?

'What is it?', I asked, a tiny bit irritated that I'd been called away at such a time.

'Sit down for a minute, love', Gran said, as Arthur went into the back garden with the paper.

'What is it?' I was concerned all of a sudden. She wanted to be alone with me. Oh God, was she ill? 'You are okay, Gran?'

'Yes, of course I am. It's nothing like that, I promise.' She smiled, as she put her hand over mine. 'Now maybe I shouldn't have interfered, and maybe you'll be cross with me', she said. 'I just wanted to do something for you. After all of the lies, you know. I thought it was about time you got to know him, and well, I knew that if I contacted him and he didn't want to know, then you wouldn't have to face the rejection. I could take it for you.'

'Dad?' I asked, as tears filled my eyes.

'Yes love. Your Dad. I searched him up. You know, on Facebook. I had to create an account and everything. Arthur helped, of course, I have no idea about such things myself, and well, he's good at things like that, isn't he?'

'Yes, he is.' I could hardly bring myself to look up at her. 'So, you found him then? I did find him myself a while back, just before Christmas. I just didn't feel ready you know. Maybe I was a bit scared, of the rejection like you said, and I wanted to enjoy the holidays without worrying about him not wanting to know. I thought maybe I'd be full of regret for contacting him. Then it was the wedding, and I didn't want to ruin that for myself or you and Arthur by being all miserable, then I just sort of talked myself out of it altogether I suppose. I thought, *well I'm happy right now, why rock the boat?* I couldn't really forget about him though'

'Oh Maddie. You should have talked to me love'

'Well if I had, then you may not have contacted him, and I'm hoping you're not going to say he didn't want to know. You're not are you?' I was suddenly filled with fear that actually that was exactly what she was going to say. Why would he want to know now, if he hadn't wanted to so far?

'Quite the opposite. I wasn't quite sure how to approach him, you know? What does one say in such situations? So, I just told him what had happened, how Emma was gone and everything. Can you believe it, he actually had no idea? He was quite devastated.'

'He didn't know what happened to her?' How could he not?'

'Well no, you see he just cut himself off completely. He wasn't on speaking terms with his family, so he had no reason to come back to England.'

'He had me. Wasn't I a reason?', I asked as my heart sank.

'Oh love', Gran said, as she put her hand on my shoulder and squeezed gently. 'Of course you were. He's never stopped wondering about you. Thinks about you all the time, he said. And I have to say I believe him, too. He was just so ashamed of what he did, he couldn't face it really. Sort of tried to convince himself that you were better off without him, and as he said, nobody had ever tried to trace him, so he thought let sleeping dogs lie and all that.'

'Well how could anyone? He didn't leave a forwarding address or anything. What was anyone supposed to do?' I said, with actual tears falling onto my cheeks. 'That's just an excuse, don't you think?', I said, looking at her for reassurance that it wasn't. 'Does he want to see me?'

'Yes, he does love. The rest is up to you. He understands if you aren't ready to see him just yet, though.'

'I don't know.' I really didn't. Part of me was thrilled at the prospect of meeting him, but then part of me was terrified that we'd have nothing in common and that, when it came to it, I'd resent him for what he did.

'Well, you don't have to know, not just yet', Gran said. 'Take your time. He's not going anywhere. Anyway, he wrote you this', she said, taking a white envelope from her bag. 'I've been walking around with this bloody thing for days', she said, as she handed it to me.

'Oh', I replied, staring at it. 'I'm scared to read it.'

'Again, take your time. No hurry. Put it to one side until you're not so scared. He's going to wait for you. He won't bother you. He promised.'

I leant into her and rested my head on her shoulder as tears fell silently. Mine and hers.

# Chapter Twenty-Six

*Dear Maddie,*

*Where do I start? There's nothing I can say that will ever make up for the way I treated your Mum. I won't try and justify it because, quite simply, there is no justification.*

*I made an enormous mess of everything. Since I spoke with Louise, I wonder if I'd stayed, would she still be alive. I'm sure you've wondered the very same thing.*

*I'm so sorry, Maddie. Sorry for leaving Emma, and sorry for leaving you. More than that, I'm sorry for never being brave enough to come back for you, or to contact you. All I can promise you, is that there has never been one single day in all these years that I have not thought about you.*

*I hope that one day, you might be able to find it in your heart to forgive me. If you can, then I'd love to see you. I'll leave it up to you. I won't pressure you, and I won't be offended if you decide not to make contact with me. I will understand.*

*Yours faithfully,*

*Dad. X*

I can't explain how I felt, seeing that word. I felt as if I should be furious with him for thinking he had any right to call himself that. Was I being disloyal to Mum if I felt anything less than fury?

Somehow, though, that wasn't how I felt. I was comforted. I just wished that feeling wasn't overwhelmed by the feeling of guilt that I was being selfish for not telling him to get lost. Didn't he deserve that? Hadn't I earned the right to tell him to get stuffed?

'At the end of the day, Mads, he's your Dad, isn't he?', Josh said as we sat on his bed eating jam doughnuts. 'It's up to you, but what have you got to lose? Really, nothing.'

'But he left us, Josh. Mum died, and it might have been down to him.'

'You know that's not true, though. No-one kills themselves because they've been ditched. From what you've said, she was messed up long before that.'

'Yeah, I know that really. It's just that I feel like, she's probably looking down at me, pleading with me not to contact him or something.'

'That's bollocks. I'm sure she'd want you to know him', he said. 'Anyway, not being a twat or anything, but she's not here and you are.'

'That's a bit twattish, actually', I said, giggling.

'Sorry. It's just that I know you. You'll never leave it alone. If you don't contact him, you'll be forever thinking about contacting him. Life is short, babe. Take it from someone who knows', he said, sighing. Josh had come to regret not making more of an effort with his Dad. He was indignant for a long time. Now he was sad about it. 'Family is important. I'll never get another chance with my own Dad.'

'I know. Don't beat yourself up though. He didn't treat you all that well. You had good reason', I said, holding his sugar-coated hand. 'Don't let guilt get the better of you.'

'Practice what you preach, then', he laughed.

I knew I wanted to see him, or at least to make contact. Actually, it was all I thought about. It kept me awake at night. I'd stare at his Facebook profile over and over. I'd looked at the message button and almost clicked it loads of times. It seemed wrong to contact him that way though. It was flippant, like it wasn't important, just something I did all the time with friends. Gran had his address. If I was going to do it, I'd write him a proper letter, in my best pen, and I'd make an effort to write neatly. I'd take my time and make sure the letters didn't look like they'd been put into words by a small child.

Poor Josh, he'd had to repeat year eleven. It was shameful, he said. He'd decided to go to university after sixth form. I wasn't sure how I felt about it. I suppose I was a bit jealous. He knew what he wanted. He'd decided he wanted to be a teacher.

I knew what I wanted, too, but I felt like maybe I was deluded to think I could ever actually be a writer and make money from it. I mean, I was just me. Nobody really. What made me think I could be anything like an author? If I thought about it too much, then I could have stopped tapping my keyboard and applied to universities like everyone else was doing. I'd decided that thinking about things was a sure-fire way to convince your brain that you couldn't possibly do anything out of the ordinary.

Josh had almost two years to go before he'd be off. I was glad he was a year behind, although I didn't tell him that. At least we had lots of time before then. He might change his mind, anyway. Although that might mean he went back to his first idea, to join the RAF. That would surely be worse. Then I'd have the added worry that he might die.

'So, are you going to write to him then?', he asked as he flopped down flat onto the bed. 'You know I'll be here for you, don't you?'

'I know, thanks.'

'Take a chance on him, Mads. What do you have to lose really?'

'Nothing, I suppose.'

'Right, I mean if it doesn't work out then you still have me, your Gran, Sarah and Arthur too. That's a lot of love, Beaven', he grinned as he pulled me down next to him.

'It sure is, Howells', I said, leaning over him and kissing his lips that were lined with grains of sugar. 'Yum.'

## Chapter Twenty-Seven

I was more nervous than I had been about meeting Sarah. I was meeting my Dad for the very first time. He'd flown over especially. He was staying at the Hilton because he didn't feel it was right to stay with us. He thought it might be too much for me, and he was probably right. I was beside myself with terror. I almost ran away twice. I thought he wasn't going to show up, because he was almost twenty minutes late, only he wasn't. I got the time wrong. I thought it was one, but it was one thirty. I was so relieved when I checked his text. How awful would it have been if hadn't turned up, if he'd had cold feet at the last minute?

My heart was beating so loudly, I felt that everyone must be able to hear it. I thought I was going to throw up. There I was, sitting alone in Starbucks, waiting to meet my Dad. I had an actual Dad, one that had flown half way around the world to meet me. I hoped he wouldn't be disappointed. What if I wasn't what he was expecting? What if…

Before I could over-think it any longer, I looked up. 'Hi.'

'Maddie, hi', he said, smiling at me. 'God, I don't know what to do', he said with a slow Australian accent. I hadn't spoken to him before. I didn't have the nerve to talk to him over the phone. It was all via text. *Of course he was going to be Australian*. It wasn't like with Penny's brief Australian phase, he'd been living there for years. It was just not something I'd thought about, and it unnerved me a little bit. 'Can I give you a hug?', he asked as I stood to greet him.

'Um, yeah I guess.'

He looked relieved as he held me. It wasn't a long hug, just enough. I felt a bit strange about it though. I went red and didn't know where to look when I sat down again. I didn't want to make him feel awkward by being all embarrassed or anything.

'Have you been here long? Shit, I'm not late, am I?' He asked looking at his phone. 'It was one-thirty right?'

'Yes, I just got here too early. I thought it was one.'

'Oh no, so you've been here all this time thinking I wasn't coming maybe', he said, looking mortified. 'So sorry.'

'No, no I checked your last text, so I knew you would be here. Well, I didn't know for sure… I just thought…' I was stuttering.

'I know what you meant. There was no way in hell that I wasn't going to be here, Maddie', he said, looking into my eyes and fixing his stare for a few seconds. I could tell he was fascinated with me.

As we drank our lattes, chatting became easy. He apologised because he kept staring at me. He said he couldn't help it. I didn't mind. I was his daughter and he probably saw himself in me. I definitely saw myself in him. He was handsome, in a rugged sort of way. His skin was tanned, and he had one of those closely shaven beards. Josh was trying to grow one, but it just came out all patchy and made him look scruffy. Adam suited it.

As the time went on, it got easier and easier. I found I really liked him and I could tell he liked me too. He told me he married Katrina five years ago. They didn't have any kids because she was a doctor and wasn't willing to give up her career. She'd told him that from the start and he was glad of it. He said he didn't want any more children because he felt like he didn't deserve any.

'Don't be silly', I said when he told me. 'Maybe you will now we've met?'

'No, not now. I'm settled. Katrina is a workaholic. She has no interest in having a family. Anyway, I have you now. I do, don't I?', he said.

'Yes, you do', I replied. He did. He was everything I could have hoped for. I hoped Mum would understand, if she was looking down at us. Gran said she would. She said, she didn't have a vindictive bone in her body. She'd want me to be happy, and if he made me that way, then she'd be thrilled. I didn't think Gran was lying.

Over the next two weeks, we saw lots of each other. We went for dinner, we went for more coffee, we went to the cinema. We went to the zoo! Yes, really. Dad said he'd always dreamt of taking me. So, I said 'Okay, let's do it'.

'Really?', he said, not sure if I was joking or not.

'Really, Dad.' It was the first time I'd called him that. He looked at me for a second and smiled. He didn't make a big deal of it or anything. After that, I said it all the time. He was my Dad.

When it came time for him to go, I was gutted. 'We'll keep in touch, won't we?'

'What sort of an idiot question is that?', he laughed. 'Of course we will. You'll be sick of me before long.'

'Shouldn't think so.'

Arthur drove him to the airport. I didn't go. I couldn't face an emotional goodbye, and to be honest, I didn't think he could either.

I sat on my bed that night wondering how it had happened. It seemed like yesterday. I barely remembered all the stuff in-between Gran telling me she'd contacted him and me meeting him. It was like time had all rolled into one, like it had all happened at the same time.

I hadn't had a Dad, and now I did. I laid back and pushed my head into my pillows. I had an actual real-life Dad. He was Dad to me. Two weeks was all that it had been, and it was like I'd known him all my life. I seemed to be over the guilt issue now. Well, I hoped I was. Maybe it would creep up on me one day, after the euphoria of it started to wear off. I really hoped it wouldn't, though. I liked this feeling. It wasn't like Gran and

Arthur weren't enough for me or anything like that. I just felt... complete, I suppose, well almost. Perhaps there was always something you couldn't have or weren't meant to have.

# Chapter Twenty-Eight

*I can't believe she has gone. She wasn't even that old. It isn't fair. It was so sudden. I've had no time to get used to the idea. One minute she was there, the next she wasn't. Arthur said it was better that way, he wouldn't have wanted to see her suffer, and I suppose he was right.*

*A massive heart-attack. They said she wouldn't have known much about it, but I'm not sure. Nobody was there with her, so we'll never know. I hope she didn't suffer alone. The thought of her being there, knowing she was probably dying, makes my stomach turn over.*

*The house feels different somehow, now she isn't in it. It is like part of it has gone with her. Poor Arthur. She didn't get around to changing her will, and she left the house to me officially. I would never try to enforce that, and anyway Dad said, legally, it's probably his right to stay. I don't care about legally. I wouldn't want it any other way.*

*Although Arthur says he may not stay. He kept his house and rented it out. He thinks he* might go back. He really wants me to have this place. I don't want him to go. I want him to stay here. I can't move back from London. I love it there, but to come back here some weekends, would be lovely. If Arthur goes, it would be like everything has changed.

I still haven't quite got used to not having her here. The funeral is tomorrow. That will make it real. She is gone, and she is never coming back. It's a weird feeling, to know you'll never see someone you loved so much, ever again. Arthur said we will see her someday, but I don't believe in heaven or anything like that, so we probably won't. He's handling it very well. He's not the most emotionally charged person at the best of times, so I hope he isn't keeping it all inside. I told him to talk to me if he needs to, but he said he doesn't.

I'm so glad Dad is here. It's like we were never apart. Every time I see him, it's as if he was there all along.

We went through all of the old photos last night. There were loads of Mum. It was the first time I'd looked at them. I'd meant to, but every time Gran suggested it, I'd chickened out. Now it seemed like the right time.

**You okay? X**

*Josh is in his final year at Plymouth University. We split briefly about a year ago. Mainly because we hardly saw each other, and I was pissed off with the situation. It seemed I was constantly battling with the life I had and the one I wanted. But there's something about us. It's like we're drawn to each other. We can never be apart for long. It wasn't as if it was jealousy or anything. He started dating someone on his course. I felt a bit weird about it, but I was determined to let him get on with it. I couldn't very well finish with him and then get all cross with him for seeing someone else. He finished it after a couple of months because, as he put it, she wasn't me.*

'I want us back Mads' Josh said to me one Saturday afternoon while we were having lunch at The Kings Head. We'd kept in touch after the split. I think we both knew it was only temporary.

'Me too', I pulled his face to mine without hesitation, planting a long soft kiss on his lips. I'd been aching to do it for weeks. I wasn't sure if he was the one, I didn't even know if there was such a thing. 'What if it doesn't work out?' I said.

'Then it doesn't, no good reason not to try though'


I had reconciled with the fact that I'd never get a publishing deal at that point. I'd been sending manuscripts off for a couple of years. It was soul destroying. I had a couple of 'nearly's, but they both came to nothing in the end. I didn't know it would be so tough. I was so happy with what I'd produced, but I started to think that maybe I wasn't as good as I thought I was.

I was working at Caltherton College in administration. It was okay, but not what I wanted. I thought it would be a stop gap until I became a full-time writer. It had become familiar, safe. There was a time when that would not have been good enough for me. Now I was beginning to think it was. Still, there was this niggling voice inside of me. *Don't give up Maddie*, it said. I wanted to shut it up for good, because it was obviously just goading me to lose the plot completely. I still had the website, but it was ticking along without too much input from me. Maybe I ought to concentrate on that I thought. Maybe get some more publicity. Forget about the writing thing once and for all. Who was I kidding to think I was ever going to be published? I said to myself.

Josh and I had been talking about booking a holiday. I wanted to go to New York, but we just couldn't afford it, so we'd downgraded to Spain for a week. We were just about to book it when my phone rang.

'Hello', I said, impatiently. Panicking that the one we'd chosen would go if we didn't click book now right away.

'Maddie Beaven?', she said.

'Yes', I said, even more irritated. It was bound to be a sales call. My contract was nearly up.

'My name is Lucinda Cartwright. I'm an agent at Miller and Falconer. You sent your manuscript to us a few weeks ago.'

'Oh yes, I did', I said, my attention quickly switching to the call. I tried not to sound too expectant. She was probably going to tell me it was good, but not quite good enough this time.

'Well I'd really like to meet up with you, Maddie. I love the way you write and I'd very much like to represent you. Can you come to London next week?'

Could I? Of course I bloody could. Apart from a tragic accident, nothing could stop me. Yes, of course', I replied.

I got my publishing deal six months later. It was a long six months, and I had started to wonder if Lucinda would ever find a publisher to take a chance on me. I didn't tell anyone at work, just in case it never happened, and they thought I'd made the whole thing up.

*I never thought I'd be living in London, working on my second book. Okay, I'm sharing a house with four other people. But that's okay. Lisa and Mel are hardly ever there, Paul locks himself away in his room most of the time and Daniel does all the cooking.*

I had been really worried about leaving Gran's. Not because I was scared of going it alone, but because I thought she might think

I was deserting her. She didn't. She was super excited for me.

'Oooh, Maddie, a proper author! I'm so pleased for you, love. You go out there and do it for the Beavens', she said, hugging me tight.

*Remembering that day fills me with sadness now. It was a happy day, everyone was happy for me. Maybe in time I'll think differently about it.*

*'Maddie!', Dad calls to me.*

*'Yes.'*

*'There's someone here to see you', he shouts.*

*'Who?'*

*'Come and see.'*

*I hoist myself from my bed, still only half awake. Who is calling on me? Maybe Penny or Darcie. I shouldn't think so. I hardly see them these days and I thought Penny was in Cornwall because she posted a load of pictures of her and Mitch on the beach with her brother's kids yesterday. I wasn't in the mood for talking, to be honest. I was tired. I'd been thinking about curling up under the* duvet and grabbing a couple of hours, actually.

'Hey Maddie'

'Sophie.'

'Long time, no see', she says, smiling up at me from the foot of the stairs. She looks exactly the same, maybe a bit fuller in the face, but apart from that she hasn't changed. 'Really sorry to hear about your Gran, Mads', she says as I get to the bottom of the stairs. 'She was lovely.'

'Yes, she was. Are you back for a visit then?', I ask, as I don't even try to stop a tear from falling down onto my cheek and into my mouth.

'Mum came back. Didn't work out with Marcus. She didn't move back to Caltherton, but not far. Cheston.'

'Oh right. They have good pubs there.' I smile, wiping my face.

'Yeah they do! Anyway, fancy grabbing a coffee somewhere? If you have time of course. I was going to come to the funeral too.'

'Were you? Oh, that's great. Really good of you.'

'Not really. I always liked her. She was good to me. Part of my life for a long time', she says, touching my arm.

'Coffee would be lovely.' I smile. 'Sophie...'

'Yes'

'I'm so sorry for what I did, you know? I always wanted to tell you that, but I was too stubborn.'

'Yeah, you were', she laughs. 'Don't worry about it. We were young. Thanks for saying that though', she smiles and gives me a huge hug. I grip her tight. My Sophie is here.

**Does magic exist, or was it all a figment of my over-active imagination? I choose to believe it does, because believing there's something more than we can see gives me hope that anything is possible. Perhaps it's science after all, the weird crazy kind that we'll never fully understand. All I know is that I have the life I dreamed of, and I did it all by wishing for it.**

Printed in Great Britain
by Amazon